DEAD TO RIGHTS

Mackenzie Owens Mystery #1

JASMINE WEBB

Prologue

I WAS THIRTY-ONE YEARS OLD THE FIRST TIME someone tried to murder me. And okay, that on its own wasn't an especially surprising fact. But I never expected that the person trying to kill me would be my own grandmother.

I had just stepped over the threshold of my new home when, out of the corner of my eye, I spotted movement. Someone was in the house, and they were swinging some sort of heavy object down toward my head. I instantly dropped to the ground and screamed, the object hitting my suitcase with a heavy thwack.

"What the fuck?" I screamed as I leapt to my feet and ran farther into the house. The smartest move ever? No, probably not. In hindsight, I would have been much better off going back the way I'd come. But look, when someone's trying to kill you, your decision-making isn't always top-notch. Trust me on this one.

I scanned the room to find something to defend myself with as I heard my attacker's footsteps behind me. Had this all been a trap? An elaborate ruse to get me to England so that I could be murdered and my body disposed of without my family and friends back in America finding out about it?

Was this what those TikTok videos warning me about my cart being marked in a Walmart had been telling me about? Was I about to be trafficked?

Not if I could help it.

Once, a long time ago, I read advice online that said that if you're being attacked, the best thing to do is to make them think you're crazy. Well, I'd become straight-up *unhinged* if it meant upping the odds of saving my life.

I ran to the bookshelf at the far end of the room and began grabbing books at random, hurling them at my attacker as hard as I could while screaming my head off.

I continued to throw the contents at my attacker, until I reached the far wall. A floor lamp stood there, and I grabbed it, immediately spinning around, doing my best Kylo-Ren-with-a-lightsaber impression.

We'll ignore the part where he dies. I was obviously way better with my makeshift weapon.

"I'm using the force, bitch!" I shouted as I hit my attacker on the arm.

"Then why don't you make like Luke

Skywalker and get the fuck off my planet? Or my house. Whichever one is fine with me," my attacker spat back at me, wincing with pain where my makeshift lightsaber had landed.

I paused as I realized it wasn't a man at all. It was a woman. An old woman. And she was holding two kitchen knives, one in each hand, standing in some sort of kung fu pose like a wannabe Bruce Lee.

"Your house? Okay, lady. I don't know what nursing home lost you on the weekly field trip to the mall, but why don't you put those knives down? This is my house, and I'm sure we can find yours again, no problem."

Shit. Who was I even supposed to call about a lost senior in my home? The police, I guess. They'd hopefully know where she belonged. I'd probably have felt pretty bad for her if it hadn't been for the whole attempted murder thing.

Right now, though, the priority was making sure those knives ended up on the floor. Or literally anywhere that wasn't inside my body.

"Nursing home? Who do you think you are? Some entitled kid who grew up on participation trophies and thinks the world owes her? So you thought you'd come over here, get rid of some weak old hag, and take over her home? Well, I have news for you: if you keep this up, you're going into the ground long before I am."

"Are you threatening me?" Wow, this lady was nuts.

"I'm defending my home. How is it that you Americans say? Standing my ground."

"Look, just put the knives down, okay? We can talk this out. We'll figure out where you live, and you'll be able to enjoy a nice cup of tea, curled up at home, in a few hours, okay?"

"The only way that's happening is if I'm using your bleeding corpse as an ottoman."

There were probably some mental health problems at play here. Maybe some dementia. But a couple attempts at niceness were about all I had in me. I was jet-lagged, I had just landed in a new country, and all I wanted to do was curl up in bed in my nice new home. Instead, I found myself being threatened by someone who looked old enough to have been best friends with William the Conqueror.

"This home is mine. I know your generation is used to taking all the property for nothing, but that's not how this works. My dad died, he left me this place, and you're trespassing on *my* property. And any chance I'd take pity on you flew out the window when you tried to kill me and then shot off into outer space when you said you were going to drink a cup of tea over my corpse. Do you really think you can kill me? You're, like, ninety years old. All I have to do is poke you with this lamp, and you're probably going to fall over and break your hip."

"You really wanna take that bet, girlie?" the old lady asked, shooting me a deranged grin.

There was something familiar about it. Maybe I'd just seen *The Dark Knight* too many times.

"Bring it on, grandma," I replied, narrowing my eyes.

"This was my son's house. I don't care what sob story you've made up, but you're not getting Carl's home."

She launched at me then, and I let out a yelp as I lunged at her with the lamp, using it like it was one of those lances from a medieval joust. I caught her square in the stomach, but that didn't stop her. She knocked the lamp aside and came after me.

I swung it hard, moving to the side to avoid the slash of her knife. "Did you say Carl?" I shouted as she slammed into the bookcase, hard, a couple of tomes falling to the ground from the force of it.

"Yes. That was my son's name. Why?"

"That's the name of my dad, the guy who left me this place."

The two of us stared at each other for a minute. If this lady was really crazy, how did she know my dad's name?

"Carl Summers?" we both asked simultaneously.

"Impossible. Carl didn't have a kid," the old lady said.

"Well, he sure as shit wasn't a dad. But he was a sperm donor. And a house donor."

"I don't believe you. I've seen these things on

the internet. People pretending to be someone else, going around scamming people, stealing their homes."

I rolled my eyes. "I have all the documents in my suitcase—which now has a nice slash in it thanks to your knife."

The lady held up a threatening blade. "I'll go have a look."

"What, and have you tear the paper up the instant you find it? Not a chance. I'll get the papers."

I carefully stepped across the room, still holding the floor lamp like a weapon in front of me, never showing my back to the crazy old lady.

Was she telling the truth? If so, that meant she actually *was* my grandmother.

No wonder that deranged grin looked so familiar. It was the same one I had.

I reached my suitcase and felt around with one hand, never lowering my weapon.

The old lady kept an eye on me, her guard up as well. "What's your name, then?" she finally asked me. "If you're going to claim to be my granddaughter, I might as well know who you are."

"Mackenzie Owens. You?"

"Margaret Summers. How old are you?"

"Thirty-one. How old are you?"

"Don't you know it's rude to ask a lady her age?"

"Yeah, but you're no lady. Besides, it's the twenty-first century. You're allowed to be over thirty now without people scurrying away from you in fear of catching wrinkles." I found the papers and grabbed them. "Here. This shows the property is mine."

"Okay. We look at them together. I'll drop the knives if you drop the lamp."

If it came down to a fistfight, my grandmother or not, I could take her.

"Fine. On the count of three. One, two, three."

Neither one of us moved, and I tilted my head to the side. "Don't you trust your granddaughter?"

"Don't you trust your grandmother?"

"You literally just tried to kill me. What do you think?"

The two of us stared each other down. "All right, fine," Margaret eventually said. "I'll put down the knives."

She slowly knelt and placed the two knives at her feet.

"I'll drop this, then," I said. "And we both step away from our weapons."

This must have been what hostage trade-offs during the Cold War were like. Slowly, I put the lamp down, and the two of us stepped away from our weapons, one step at a time, neither breaking eye contact.

After four steps, I nodded. "Okay. Come here, and you can look at my papers."

I was near a desk by the front window, so I put the papers there as Margaret came over and spoke. "These are from the same law firm I spoke to. I have a copy that looks exactly like this. Where did you get these?"

"They were mailed to me three weeks ago," I said. Inside, my heart began to sink. What if this was all a horrible mistake? "I got this letter saying that my father had died and that he left me this home in his will, as I was his only child. At first, I thought it was a mistake. But then my mom told me about my dad. They had a fling when he was studying in New York for a semester abroad and she was visiting an aunt for a few months. She got pregnant, and when she told Carl, he bailed and went back to England. Mom moved back home to Seattle, had me, and we never heard from him again. The next news I got was when I received the letter from the lawyer."

"And so you came here, thinking this property was left to you."

"I did. I uprooted my whole life, and now you're telling me this was all bull? That the one thing my father ever did for me in this life was fake? That I spent thousands of dollars moving here for nothing?"

"Well, I can tell you I have a piece of paper that says the same thing as yours. It leaves this place to me, his mother. I'll tell you what: we're going to head down to the solicitor's offices this very minute and sort this all out. There's obviously been a mistake made somewhere. And when it's discovered it's on your side, you can move right on back to America and live your life."

"Oh, really? Is that how you react to finding out you've got a new granddaughter? You just want to kick her out of *her* home and send her flying back across the world, never to be seen again? I can see where Carl got his parenting skills."

"You can't possibly blame *me* for this. I've come to take over my son's home, and all of a sudden, this woman I've never heard of comes out of the woodwork, staking a claim herself and pretending to be my granddaughter? Come on, now. Forgive me for being just a *little* bit skeptical."

"Fine. We go see a lawyer. Because as we both know, lawyers always make *everything* better," I snapped.

Margaret barked out a laugh despite herself but quickly glared at me once more. "Good. We'll sort this out, and the sooner you get out of my hair, the better."

I couldn't believe this was happening.

Chapter 1

MARGARET AND I WALKED ALONG IN A FROSTY silence that was perhaps not a peace treaty between us but at the very least a cease-fire. She wasn't trying to actively kill me anymore, which was always a bonus.

How had this happened? I'd received the letter in the mail three weeks ago. My father had died and left me his home as well as the bookshop he owned. The keys to both buildings were enclosed. It was supposed to be mine. And I wasn't a *total* moron; I knew there were a ton of scams out there. So I'd done some googling. Sure enough, Carl Summers had lived in the Cornwall town of St. Albinus for the past twelve years, where he ran a local bookshop.

He had died of a heart attack two months earlier, according to the local paper, which all checked out. But why would someone run this elaborate scam to get me into a small town in

England? It just didn't make any sense. It wasn't a scam. It couldn't be. I had inherited this place, and it was all going to get sorted out.

I looked at the name on the top of the papers I'd gotten, which I still held in my hand. There was no chance in the world I was going to let go of this.

"Do you know who this is? Alfred Palmer, the lawyer?"

Margaret snorted. "Yes. He and Carl were best friends growing up. He's thick as a post and a worse lawyer than whoever failed at putting OJ Simpson behind bars. The fact that he stuffed this up is about as surprising to me as waking up and finding out the sky is blue."

"Oh, good," I muttered.

One of the advantages of St. Albinus was that nothing was far away. This place was tiny compared to Seattle, where I'd grown up. And the town center was also entirely car free, which only added to the feeling of having stepped back in time. Even the river, slowly meandering through the town from the bay around which St. Albinus was built, seemed to be treating its journey like a lazy afternoon stroll, taking its good time to get wherever it was going.

But I wasn't in a mood to appreciate the picturesque fairy-tale beauty of the village. I could do that later. After we'd sorted things out and I found out that I was, in fact, the rightful owner of the property left to me by my father.

It took us less than two minutes to walk down the street before Margaret stopped in front of a house. The two-story brick home, one in a row of about ten attached houses, was made of gray, unevenly sized bricks. White-framed divided windows on either side of the front door were lined with green vines that rose up to the second story, and small bushes separated the front of the house from the sidewalk.

Above the front door hung a sign: Alfred Palmer, Solicitor.

Margaret opened the large, modern, white front door that accented the old-style home beautifully and stormed inside. "Alfred, you fucked up, and you had better fix it," she called out into the entrance.

I couldn't help but grin as I followed her into the building. She'd tried to kill me, but honestly? I could believe she was my grandmother.

As soon as we entered, a young woman jumped up from her reception desk, panic etched on her face. "Margaret, you can't go in there," she said. "He's with a client."

"Good. Maybe if I interrupt them, it'll be too late for Alfred to ruin that person's life too," Margaret snapped at her. She stormed past the woman and through a door into an office.

I flashed the woman a "sorry, can't do anything about this" shrug and followed her.

The office was all mahogany bookshelves, matching desk, leather chairs, and dark carpeting, with a window leading to the backyard at the back of the room. The man at the desk rose quickly to his feet when we entered. He was in his fifties, and his hair had obviously abandoned him decades ago, but he refused to give up the pretense, with the few stray gray hairs he had left combed forward to give the illusion of a hairline. He was tall and slim, clean-shaven, with blue eyes and a hard mouth. He wore a black suit that stood out against his pale skin and made him look a bit more like a creepy undertaker than the local lawyer.

"Margaret," he said coolly as the client on the other side of the desk turned to see what was going on. "What a surprise. As you can see, I'm currently with a client, but Rebecca at the front can schedule an appointment for you—"

"You messed up, Alfred. If your client has any sense at all, she'll pack up and leave and go find a solicitor in a town elsewhere who understands how a will works."

Alfred coughed uncomfortably. "What seems to be the problem, Margaret? I'm sure this is all just a misunderstanding, and you've likely read a document incorrectly. We can sort this out quickly. Patricia, if you'll just excuse me for one moment."

"Don't treat me like a stupid old woman. I have more brain cells in my pinkie finger than you do in that whole head of yours."

"I don't think the pinkie has any brain cells."

"Exactly," Margaret snapped. "Now, do you want to tell me why this child here has papers telling her Carl's home has been passed down to her?"

"Who is this?" Alfred asked, looking to me confusedly.

"Mackenzie Owens," I replied. "Carl Summers's daughter."

"Oh," Alfred said, his ears going a little bit pink. "Well, I'm afraid this really is all just a misunderstanding. Yes, you both received documents saying you're half owners of the property, as that's what you are."

"Only neither one of us have documents that say that. You wrote us both a letter saying we own the property."

"If you misunderstood, I apologize—"

"Oh, I understand exactly," Maggie interrupted. "I understand that you've botched this whole thing. Now I've moved into my son's home, and his daughter, who I didn't even know existed an hour ago, shows up in my new place, claiming it's hers."

"Hey, this hasn't been a walk in the park for me, either," I shot at her. "I moved across the world for this property, and I was greeted by my grandmother trying to murder me."

"I'll just make another appointment for a later date," Patricia murmured, grabbing her bag and clutching it close to her chest as she got up from her chair and slunk out of the room.

Alfred held up his hands. "Look, obviously, somewhere along the line, someone who wasn't me made a mistake. The document should have read, to both of you, that you inherited a half interest in the property. That's what Carl's will says."

"So what happens now?" I asked. "I just uprooted my whole life to move to this country."

"And I've already sold the old cottage I used to live in."

Alfred looked from one of us to the other. "It's a three-bedroom home, not to mention ownership in the bookshop property. Why don't the two of you live together?"

"Did you miss the part where she tried to murder me half an hour ago?" I asked.

"I'm not living with her. I've lived alone for the past forty-six years. I'm not babysitting anyone anymore."

"Well, I don't know what else to tell you. Short of one of you getting a hotel or renting another property while you sort out the sale or something, there's nothing else to be done."

"This is what happens when you let people buy their way into studying law," Margaret snapped, turning to me as she motioned to Alfred. "Ridiculous. Absolutely ridiculous."

"I know this must be a frustrating situation, but there's nothing else I can do," Alfred said.

I sighed. "Okay. I've been awake for, like, twenty-four hours straight. I've travelled halfway around the world. I got into a deathmatch with my own grandmother. Can I come back to the home we're apparently sharing and just go to sleep for a while and sort this out later?"

Margaret considered my words. "Fine. And I promise I won't stab you in your sleep."

"Thank you. What a comforting thing to say."

Margaret turned to Alfred. "I want a copy of every document you have regarding my son's will in my email inbox within the next twenty minutes, or I will come back here and set you on fire."

"I would take that threat seriously," I replied. "And I would also like a copy of that email."

"Yes, yes, of course," Alfred muttered. "Rebecca will take care of that right away."

"And don't you dare try and blame this on her," Margaret warned. "I've known you your whole life, Alfred. You have the IQ of a piece of loose cardboard flying on the motorway. You messed this up, and now you've uprooted two lives. You can't expect me to live with her."

I couldn't have agreed more.

THERE WAS NOTHING MORE TO BE DONE AT Alfred's office. Obviously, he had screwed up the paperwork, and instead of being told that I owned *half* the property, I had been told the whole place was mine. It was going to have to get sorted out, but right now, I was crashing, and fast.

Margaret and I walked back to what had turned out to be our shared home.

"I can't believe that imbecile thinks the two of us are going to live together," Margaret muttered. "Utterly moronic."

"I agree," I said. "Look, you said you just sold your cottage. Can't you just buy another one or something?"

"I could if there was anything available. But the last few years, anything remotely decent has been scooped up by investors looking to turn them into holiday homes to list on Airbnb. Or they're using it as a lock up and leave. There aren't any one or two-bedroom homes for sale in St. Albinus at the moment, and should another come up, I'll likely be outbid."

"Well, I broke the lease on my apartment back in America, *and* I don't have a job anymore," I said.

"I suppose for now, there's nothing to do but make the best of it. There's still a bed in the extra bedroom. Carl used it as a guest room, so you might as well sleep there for now until we've got it all sorted."

We reached the house and entered. For the first time, I finally got a good look around. If you ignored the fact that it looked like a giraffe on cocaine had come by for a visit, it was actually quite a charming home. The honey-colored hardwood floors added warmth to the open living room. The built-in bookcases had been painted matte black and were filled with volumes, floor to ceiling. In the center was the original fireplace, framed with pale limestone.

Under the front window was a small desk, and a modern leather couch was pressed against the far wall, next to an entrance leading to the kitchen at the back of the home. Directly in front of me was a staircase, the wall next to it made of original stone, and I headed up after grabbing my suitcase.

"The first door to the right is the guest room," Margaret announced as she followed me up.

I walked in to find a decently sized, plainly furnished room. It had a queen-sized bed, and frankly, that was all I cared about right at that second.

"Bathroom is down the hall," Margaret said. "There are towels in the closet next to it."

I nodded, and Margaret left. I quickly opened my suitcase, grabbed my toiletries, had a quick shower to wash off a layer of travel grime, and collapsed into bed.

This was not how I had expected my first day in England to go.

Chapter 2

I WOKE UP TO A THIN STREAM OF LIGHT filtering in through the window. I wiped the sleep out of my eyes, and everything came flooding back to me. I'd uprooted my whole life to come inherit this property in England, and it had all gone horribly wrong.

I groaned and found my phone on the night-stand. I tapped the screen to check the time. Three-forty-seven. Jet lag was a bitch.

Rolling over, I got out of bed, stifling a yawn. Heading to the window, I looked down at the town. The moon reflected on the Morehog River in front of me like silver tinsel dancing over the black water. It was the only movement; the rest of the town was completely still.

If I looked really far to the right, I could see the vague outline of masts in the harbor, shielded from the open ocean.

This was a bit unsettling. I had always been a

city person. I had grown up in Seattle and moved to New York to start my career. The sounds of horns, sirens, and people shouting from the street were the soothing sounds that helped me drift off to sleep. Here, there was only eerie silence. But being around millions of people doesn't make you any less lonely, as it turns out.

So, I thought I would start again. That was what had brought me here. It was fate, after all. Or so I'd thought. My silly pie-in-the-sky, never-gonna-happen dream had always been to run a small bookstore. Something cozy, where I'd know all of my customers by name. Where people would feel comfortable discussing their favorites with me. Where I could recommend something that would truly make someone's day. And then it turned out my father had just such a bookstore, and he had left it to me?

Yeah, this was fate. This whole thing with Margaret was a bump in the road, but it was meant to be. No question about it. I would have my store. I would run it, and I would be good at it. I'd become friends with my customers as we discussed what Agatha Christie's best murder was. And how we'd get away with murder if we ever had to.

I'd throw in a little coffee shop so I could make my favorite—iced caramel lattes—while curling up on the comfortable armchairs with an advance copy of a book I'd been looking forward to.

I was going to be a cottagecore queen, damn it. With some cool witchy vibes to go with it. This was meant to be. I wasn't going to let a technicality ruin my dreams.

I threw on some clothes and quietly made my way downstairs. I didn't want to wake up Margaret. I headed into the kitchen and rummaged around in the cupboards, looking for coffee, but there wasn't any. And it was three in the morning. Something told me there was going to be no twenty-four-hour Starbucks in this village.

"Can I help you?" a voice said behind me.

I almost dropped the mug I was holding. "Margaret," I said, turning with a tight smile. "I didn't mean to wake you."

"I'm a light sleeper."

"Which is shocking, since you don't appear to have any coffee."

"This is England, dear. We drink tea."

"It's the twenty-first century. You can drink two things."

"I've never really been one for coffee," she said. She practically shoved me out of the way as she dragged out an old electric kettle that looked like it had probably helped send man to the moon and filled it with water. "Tea does just as well."

"Except for the supply of wakey-wakey drugs," I replied.

"I prefer to let my body keep me awake rather than relying on external stimulants."

"Congratulations, I guess."

A minute later, the kettle began screaming like a banshee. Margaret walked over and pressed the off button, and the scream turned into a shriveled squeal before dissipating completely. She poured two cups of tea and pushed one across the counter toward me. This kitchen had obviously been recently renovated; the cabinets were dark green with just a hint of blue and gold hardware. We leaned on a white quartz countertop. The backsplash was cream-colored subway tile in a herringbone pattern.

This was basically my dream kitchen. And I owned half of it.

"I was thinking," Margaret continued. She drop a couple cubes of sugar into her cup of tea and stirred it with a spoon before taking a sip and continuing. "About our conundrum."

"Yes?"

"The thing is, Mackenzie, you're abrasive."

"Thank you."

"You're welcome. I did mean it as a compliment."

Well, that I hadn't expected.

"So here is what I'm thinking: neither one of us really has a lot of options at the moment.

Alfred was right, this is a three-bedroom home. What do you do for work?"

"Graphic design and marketing."

"Well, you're not going to find many takers for a job like that here."

"I had planned on running the bookshop," I said.

Margaret gaped at me. "Do you mean that?"

"Yes. It's been my dream. Don't tell me you've got a way to screw that up for me, too."

"You don't seem to me to be very customer-service minded."

"I've never had a client come at me with two knives. I assure you, I am very good at what I do. I'm trained in marketing. I can make the book-store successful."

"Well, you'll succeed where your father failed, then. It was his stupid hobby, but he never fully got it off the ground. Anyway, as I was saying, I think Alfred's solution is the best one. We co-exist here together, at least until one of us is willing or able to find elsewhere to live."

"Fine. And neither one of us will try and kill the other?"

"Agreed. I must say, I quite like that my granddaughter has a little bit of a personality to her."

"I would say the same thing, but then I found out you don't drink coffee, and I'm not sure I can get over that," I replied.

Margaret almost cracked a smile. "You may as well call me Maggie. Everyone does."

"And I'm Mack. Like the truck."

"I assume you mean lorry, then?"

"I'll run over anyone you want."

"I don't doubt it. All right, then, it's settled. We share the home. I've taken the master bedroom, and I'm not giving it up, so you can keep the one you're in. But if you'd like to replace the furniture, I've no problem with that at all. Would you like the third bedroom?"

"I don't think so. What was in it?"

"Carl used it as a general storage space. I haven't been through his things in there. It's been... difficult."

Maggie swallowed hard, then it hit me. Up until now, we hadn't spoken about Carl at all, beyond what financial offerings he'd left us. He had been her son, whom she'd borne inside of her and raised. To me, he was just a name on a birth certificate, but to her, he would have been so much more than that.

"I'm sorry," I said. "About Carl."

"Thank you. It hasn't been easy since he passed. I know you probably don't care about him at all. It's not as though he was a presence in your life."

"You didn't know about me at all?" I asked quietly. Maggie had implied as much yesterday, but I wanted to be sure.

"No. He never mentioned you. It wasn't until

after his death that Alfred told me about you. Carl didn't want me to know, he said. But you seem to have done all right for yourself despite the lack of a father figure."

"My mom worked hard to provide for me as a single parent. Although most people would disagree with you. I was always getting in trouble at school. Apparently, my mouth speaks before my brain has the time to decide whether or not that's a good idea."

"It's only people who are too scared to tell the truth who worry about that sort of thing," Maggie replied.

"That's how I've always seen it too," I said with a small smile.

"As far as grandchildren go, I suppose you could be worse."

"Do you have any others? Grandchildren, I mean."

"No. Carl was my only child, and you're the only one he had. As far as I know, anyway. But I assume he would have named any others in the will too."

"Have you lived here your whole life?"

"Most of it, yes. I moved here with my first husband at nineteen after growing up in Truro."

"What happened to him?"

"He died. Christmas Day, 1972. I couldn't have asked for a better present from Santa."

"Well, this got dark fast. Did you kill him

27

too? There seems to be a pattern here. Am I going to end up on a true-crime podcast?"

"He slipped on a patch of ice and hit his head when he insisted on going out. His whole family can attest to the fact that I was in the living room after having told him it was too dangerous and that he really didn't need to bet on the horses on Boxing Day. But James insisted, and the universe had different plans for him."

"Was he Carl's father?"

"No. That was my second husband, Tim. I married him in 1974. I already lived here. Carl was born the year after that. He died when Carl was one."

"How?"

"He was too into coffee." Maggie obviously didn't want to talk about it.

Maggie grunted, and I cracked a smile at her moxie. "Too bad for you. Can't divorce your grandkids. By the way, tea sucks."

"That's your American upbringing. Never learned to enjoy a proper cuppa. Very disappointing. I'm not sure we'll be able to live together if you don't like tea."

"If that's a deal-breaker for you, you'd never make it these days. I once had a roommate who secretly decided to breed snakes in her room as a side hustle and didn't tell any of us. She got drunk one night, opened the terrariums to feed them, and passed out without closing them properly. You can guess how that ended."

"Did you evict her?"

"No, because she paid the rent on time, and as far as roommates go, that's far from the worst story you'll ever hear."

"Well, I've never had a roommate. I lived with my parents until I married James. Then, after his death, I lived alone in the house we owned until I married Tim. We worked hard to buy property."

"Yeah, I could have worked hard and saved too, when homes cost six dollars."

"Oh, please. It was a little bit more difficult than that."

"Your first down payment probably couldn't buy a footlong at Subway anymore. Believe me, if homes still cost the same as they did back then, I'd have one. It sounds better than finding out about your roommate's snakes at three in the morning."

"I imagine it would."

The two of us stood across from each other in frosty silence. This felt a bit like the end of the Cold War. We weren't actively trying to kill each other anymore, but there was very little trust there.

"What are your thoughts about the bookshop?" I asked.

"I haven't got any. Thought it was a waste of time. A vanity project. Carl wasn't making any money from it. He pretended otherwise, but I know the truth. It's not a real business. You ask me, you should have stayed in America, where you had a job that you say you did well. Although if you were willing to drop it to come here and run a bookshop, I'm not sure how much sense you really could have."

"If the universe drops a bookstore into your lap in the most beautiful part of England and says 'Here, this is yours now to do with what you want, oh, and you also get a house with it,' there isn't a millennial on this planet who would say no to that. I'm literally living the dream that has existed in a whole bunch of memes."

"What is a meme?"

"Do you not use the internet at all?"

"Of course I do. I'm old, not a Luddite."

"Then how do you not know what a meme is?"

"I choose not to partake in social media, as I find it to be a vain expression of self-gratification that serves no use to anybody."

"Well, you're not *entirely* wrong. But so you're not sitting there on Facebook adding a new status that just says 'how to download PDF to computer'?"

"I am not, and I'm offended you asked. I know how to use the internet."

"Questionable, since you don't know what a meme is."

"I've told you, I'm not interested."

"I'm not interested in tea, but I can still tell you're drinking Earl Grey. Just because you're not interested in something or are ignorant about it doesn't make it unimportant."

"Touché," Maggie replied.

"Anyway, a meme is a usually funny photo that works its way around the internet, often with small changes to make the meme fit the topic. And a lot have to do with having the opportunity to change your life by going somewhere romantic in a way that's completely unrealistic. Like getting left a bookstore in Cornwall, along with a house. That doesn't happen to people in real life. Most of the time. So when the universe dropped it into my lap, I figured I had to do it. When else will I ever get the opportunity to do something like this? Never. There will always be other marketing jobs. But this? No, this is once in a lifetime. The memes just never mentioned sharing with a psychopathic grandmother you didn't know you had."

"Please. I'm not a psychopath."

"You don't drink coffee. Oh, and you already tried to kill me once."

"Tea is far superior."

"So you're not going to be involved in the bookstore at all?"

"No. If it were up to me and you weren't around, I'd be closing it down permanently."

"What's wrong with it?"

"Everything. No one reads books anymore, and those that do are doing so on those newfangled e-readers or their phones."

"I don't think that's true. Sure, reading electronically is on the rise, but there are lots of people who still enjoy the smell of a fresh paperback. The sound of flipping through the pages of a new purchase. The slightly grainy feel of the paper beneath their fingertips."

"Well, even if you're right, the problem Carl had was he thought he was in Central London. Honestly, you've never seen a more boring selection of books in your life. It was as though he simply went through the *Sunday Times* every week and ordered every book that's on the bestsellers list without bothering to look at any others. Bestsellers only."

I nodded. "There's no way that would work here. This is a small village, a cozy town, that requires a more curated touch."

"Precisely right."

"Where did the money come from for Carl to start his business? And why did he do it?"

"He trained in finance and worked in the City in London. He moved back here to be with his childhood friends. He told me he grew tired of the fast-paced life in the City and wanted to come homes. Put all of his money into the bookshop, thinking it would be a hit. It wasn't."

"It was losing money?"

"I assume you know virtually nothing about my son's finances?"

"No. Only that I own half of this house and bookstore."

"There was almost nothing else. If he hadn't died, I expect this next year would have been his last in business. He'd have found himself with no other choice but to close up shop and to move back to London. It's why I think you should give up before you start, frankly. The store is a money pit. Save yourself what little you have left. It might be nice to dream of a romantic life on the internet, but reality is quite a bit different."

I shrugged. "It's not like I have anything else to do. I might as well give it a shot. I didn't see much of the village yesterday, but I get the impression marketing specialists with a degree in graphic design aren't in very high demand around here."

"No, you aren't wrong. All the same, there are better ways to spend your time than to essentially light what little money you have on fire."

"I could always spend it all on avocado toast instead," I replied.

Maggie cracked a smile. "As far as I'm concerned, it's all yours. But don't get your hopes up. Do you know where the shop is located?"

"I'm told its right in the center of town."

"Exactly. I haven't been there since he passed, but you would have been sent a key. It's yours to do with as you wish."

Chapter 3

A FEW HOURS LATER, WHEN THE SUN CAME UP, I got changed and left the house to explore St. Albinus and finally get a look at the new bookstore I was going to run.

I grabbed Maggie's phone number before I left, just in case. Not like I was going to get lost in a town this size. It was more like a village. There couldn't have been more than four thousand people living in this place. Plymouth was the closest thing to a city in the immediate area, and even it only had a couple hundred thousand people, according to the Google search I had done before hopping onto the plane. And even then, it was a two hour drive away.

Oh well, at least London was only about six hours away by train if I started to really miss civilization. But as soon as I stepped outside, I was enchanted. Carl's home—my home—exited onto River Way, so named because it looked directly onto the Morehog River, which slowly meandered along in a curving path. To the left, it continued as far as the eye could see, while to the right, heading downtown, it soon reached St. Albinus harbor, the protected bay on which the town was built. A low stone wall, about a foot high, prevented the most obvious falls into the water. But given that the crystal water seemed to be barely more than two feet deep, I figured drowning wasn't a big issue here. Beneath my feet were light-beige, well-worn cobblestones, smooth from centuries of people walking over them, treading the same path I now did.

On the far side of the river was an expansive park that led toward the cliffs that dropped off into the ocean.

This was perfection.

I turned to the right and walked along the road toward Wharf Road and the center of town. A low, arched bridge made of stone crossed the river not far from home, leading to a well-used dirt path into the park on the other side. I walked past the idiot solicitor's office and continued along the river as it turned the corner, quickly finding myself on Wharf Road, the obvious center of town.

It began at the far end of the bay and continued all the way along the expanse. It was the main commercial street in town, passing by the harbor filled with boats and then turning into a beautiful, protected beach. Across from the beach, Wharf Road went from being a single-lane, pedestrian-only avenue to a large square, opening up into a community hub.

Benches surrounded large boxes of flowers, which were still hiding away this early in the morning. Strings of triangular Union Jacks strung high between buildings danced in the early-morning breeze. High, old-fashioned streetlamps lit all of Wharf Road with a warm glow. The main square comprised at least ten, maybe twelve shops. The buildings here were all either one or two stories high, with apartments above many of the storefronts overlooking the water. Most had planters hanging from the windows, the vibrant colors of the flowers contrasting beautifully with the light-colored limestone bricks. A few of the businesses used both levels, with restaurants offering ocean views from the top floor.

Most of the businesses were still shuttered for the night, their windows dark. But I spotted a single A-frame sign at the front of a building on the far end of the square. Two large bay windows between the door emanated a warm, inviting glow against the still-dark and sleepy exterior. A sign above the door, in a simple but elegant serif font, read "The Ugly Mug Café."

Ugly or not, I'd drink out of a trough right now if it came with enough caffeine to keep a sloth on Xanax awake.

I stepped inside and found myself in a beautiful, cozy café. Directly in front of me was a long wooden counter on which sat dozens of cakes, cookies, pies, buns, and every sweet under the sun I could possibly imagine. Each wall was lined with a long wooden bench topped with a heather-gray cushion, interspersed with tables. The chairs facing the benches were all painted white, brightening up the space. Free-floating wooden shelves on the wall held small pots of flowers, lit candles, and small bags of coffee beans.

Oh, and all sorts of obviously handmade mugs with all sorts of strange designs. One had a face that could best be described as "SpongeBob after twenty years of hardcore meth use." Another was shaped like an upside-down amanita mushroom, with the actual mug being the beige stem and the cap acting as a kind of built-in plate. A third one, which I was pretty sure was supposed to be a cat, looked like the pottery cup I'd made for my mom as part of a third-grade art project.

Even at eight years old, it had been obvious I was not going to be the next Michelangelo.

At the counter, a woman about my age with bright-pink hair in a pixie cut grinned at me. She had on a plain black polo with a black apron over the top, "The Ugly Mug Café" printed across the front. "First time, babes?" Her accent was a little bit different to Maggie's, and that of the lawyer we saw the other day.

I smiled back. "Am I that obvious?"

"Yes. But to be fair to you, most people are. Let me guess: just come off the plane from America."

"You got it," I said, walking up to the counter, my eyes immediately drawn to the hand-painted chalkboard menu on the back wall.

"It's the jet lag that gives you away. No one else in this place under the age of sixty is up until at least nine o'clock. When did you land?"

"Yesterday morning. And I had a day."

"How long are you here for?"

"Permanently. Or so I hope."

The woman raised her eyebrows. "Working?"

"Yeah. You know the bookstore?"

"The one owned by Carl Summers?"

"That's the one. I own it now. I'm his daughter."

The woman let out a low whistle. "Daughter? Seriously?"

"Yup. It was a surprise to me too."

"You've just given me *the* best gossip this place has heard in, I dunno, probably a century at this point, babes. Carl Summers has a daughter, and she's come to take over the bookshop. You've got your work cut out for you there, let me tell you."

"What's wrong with it? Maggie's given me an idea of what to expect, but I haven't been in there yet. She doesn't have any coffee at home, so I figured I'd load up on some caffeine before I check it out."

"It's just boring. That's the biggest problem with the place. Well, that, and Carl didn't have a clue what he was selling. I'm pretty sure he read four books in his life."

"Why'd he open the shop, then?"

The barista hoisted a single shoulder skyward. "Beats me. Rich guy from the City with more money than sense who wants a hobby? Sorry, I know he was your dad and all."

"Don't worry about it. I never knew the guy. He ran off on my mom as soon as he found out she was pregnant."

"Ah, a real gentleman. But hey, you got a shop out of it. Where are you staying, then? I know Maggie got the house. I thought she got the shop too."

"It's, uh, being sorted out at the moment. Technically, the house and the shop were left to both of us."

"Oh, good, an inheritance squabble. Well, you being here alone is going to get some tongues wagging. Just be ready for that. You from a small town?"

I shook my head. "City, through and through."

"Then this place is going to be a change for you. Don't be surprised if people look at you like you've grown three heads. Or if they start asking questions you find way too invasive. That's just how it is in small towns."

"Did you grow up here?"

"Nope. Born and raised in London, which is how I know what a change this is."

"What made you choose here?"

"I don't like the city. There's too much noise. There are too many people. I constantly felt like my brain was so busy taking everything in that I couldn't hear myself think. Whereas out here, everything moves at a slower pace. Our customers are either the tourists who are looking for a relaxing repose away from their day-to-day lives and aren't worried about whether they're going to make their next meeting or the locals who live here because of the lifestyle Cornwall offers. Either way, no one is moving at a break-neck pace."

"Right. If this was New York, I'd already have ten people behind me in line, screaming at me to order or get lost," I said with a grin. "Seattle isn't quite as bad, but people would totally be passively-aggressively glaring at me. I'm Mack, by the way."

"Sophie."

I ordered an iced caramel latte—my main vice—and Sophie rang up the order. "Can I tempt you with some of these delicious goodies? The owner's wife cooks them herself out the back. On the house."

"Well, how can I say no to that?" I replied

with a smile, my mouth watering as I took in the multitude of options. There were cinnamon buns slathered with rich frosting. Cream-colored muffins dotted with thick, juicy blueberries and crispy streusel topping. Chocolate cake layered with creamy white frosting, naked-style, topped with fresh berries. And about twenty other options.

As soon as my eyes landed on the New York–style cheesecake, covered with a gorgeous strawberry glaze, I knew there was no hope for me. I was a sucker for cheesecake. Sophie packed it up for me in a nice compostable container, with a compostable fork to go with it, and began making my coffee.

"You'll have to come in and stay for a drink one day. You haven't had a true experience here until you've had a coffee from one of our mugs. Some of them literally give me nightmares."

I laughed. "Where do they come from?"

"The original batch was bought as a prank by the owner, who found them in the back of an antiques shop in Birmingham. He started serving from them, and the whole thing took on a life of its own. Now, we get people from around the world who send us every ugly mug they can find. Some of them are frankly horrifying. There's one of Boris Johnson somewhere, and the potter added straw to the rim of the mug to make his hair."

"Nightmare fuel."

"Agreed. Anyway, here's your coffee, in a very normal take-away cup. Do stop by again, especially if you're a morning person. We open at seven every day."

"I'll come back for sure. Thanks for this, Sophie. It was nice to meet you."

"You as well. And good luck with the bookshop. It could be something great."

"I think so," I said with a smile. I left the coffee shop and took a big sip of the delicious coffee through the straw, the nutty roast mingling beautifully with the sweet caramel syrup.

Anyone who thought tea was better than this was insane.

The bookshop, as it turned out, was just off the square, down Wharf Road, the street lined with even more shops for tourists to enjoy.

A minute later, I was standing in front of St. Albinus Books. That was the first thing that was going to have to go: the name. It was as boring as the exterior. Seriously. The gorgeous wood on the outside framing the large windows had been painted a plain gray that evoked the color of the sky in Seattle between November and April. The large windows had been covered up with newspaper, but there was promise here. If I repainted the wood framing, it could be really cute. The windows offered plenty of space to display cool books and would let in tons of natural light.

Maggie and Sophie were both right. Cornwall obviously had an energy of its own. This wasn't the place to hawk the latest bestsellers off the charts. This was the kind of place where people would come to find a book they'd never heard of but that would be exactly what they needed at that time. A book that made them laugh or cry or change their life.

Yes, I was going to transform this place into the perfect cozy Cornwall nook.

Taking a deep breath, I did my best impression of a Charlie Chaplin sketch as I tried to get my keys out of my bag while not tipping over my coffee or dropping my delicious slice of cheesecake. Even the key to this place was adorable, one of those large antiques that looked like it would open a treasure chest hidden away for hundreds of years.

I expected the key to turn firmly in the lock, but it was smooth, and I didn't feel a thing. Maybe the security here was a bit more modern than I thought, and the key was just for show.

Turning the handle, I entered the bookstore, expecting to see my future. Expecting to see what I could do to transform this into a haven for bibliophiles.

Instead, I opened the door and found myself looking down at a body on the floor.

Chapter 4

I LET OUT A YELP, DROPPING THE CONTAINER carrying the cheesecake. I immediately closed the door, then looked up and down the street as if to see whether anyone had noticed what had just happened. As if I'd killed the guy. Ridiculous.

"Get it together, Mack," I whispered to myself. I reopened the door, and my eyes fell to the cake on the floor. Luckily, while the top of the container had popped open, the cake was still sitting in it, none the worse for wear. I quickly picked it up then looked at the body on the ground in front of me.

Hey, priorities.

I inhaled sharply as I looked at the man. The person lying in the middle of the floor was probably in his fifties. Something like that? It was a lot harder to gauge the age of dead people, I'd just realized. That was when it hit me: I wasn't a hundred percent sure he was dead yet. But the pool of blood around him was a pretty good indicator.

Still, I had to be sure. I placed my coffee and cake on a shelf next to the door and carefully crept over to the man. I closed my eyes as I pressed two fingers against his neck, but his skin was colder than a brass bra doing push-ups in the snow. There was no doubt about it. He was dead.

I pulled out my phone and called Maggie. I didn't know what else to do.

"Don't tell me you've got lost in a two-street village," she answered.

"Don't tell me you're the one who left a body in your son's bookshop," I replied.

For what I assumed was the first time in her life, Maggie was left speechless on the other end of the line. "What?" she finally said after a couple of seconds had passed.

"Someone's been murdered in the bookshop. I'm staring at the body right now. Did you put it there?"

"Why would you ask me that?"

"It's your son's bookshop, and you're the most murderous person I've met in England so far."

"Are you sure he's dead?"

"Real sure. And you're avoiding the question. You didn't put him here, did you?"

"Of course I didn't. Stay there. I'll be there in two minutes."

"Should I call the police?"

"Not until I've had a look. And even then, what are they going to do? Don't touch *anything*, you hear me?"

"Well, I was planning on bathing in the blood on the floor, but now that you tell me that…"

"How on earth did I end up with a grand-daughter who's got as much of a mouth as I do?" Maggie grumbled, then she hung up on me.

I sighed and figured there was nothing to do but wait. The dead man was dressed nicely. Business pants and a button-up shirt. How had he gotten here? Who was he?

The cause of death was immediately obvious. When I moved to the side, I could just make out the handle of a knife sticking out from underneath him. I wasn't about to flip the body over, but it didn't take a genius to figure out the pool of blood had probably come from a stab wound.

A minute later, the door opened, and Maggie walked in. Her eyes immediately fell to the body on the floor. "You weren't kidding."

"About there being a dead person here? No, I wasn't. Is that the kind of thing you normally prank people with?"

"You never know with you young people today"

"Do you know who he is?"

"I do, actually. One of the worst people in town. I guess someone decided to take karma into their own hands. Gregory Hamlisch. He's a con artist, essentially. Whatever low-level scummy plot he had going on must have finally caught up to him."

"So, uh, we have to call the cops, right? We can't just leave him here."

"I suppose so. I'll do it. Just a warning: the local sergeant, who will be in charge of the investigation here, is a complete and utter donut. In every sense of the word. Don't believe for a second that he'll do anything other than bungle this entire investigation. You cannot trust him."

"I don't trust a lot of people," I replied quietly.

"Good." Maggie pulled out her phone and dialed a number.

While she spoke, I glanced around the rest of the store. I tried not to feel too sorry for myself and how all of this was affecting me. After all, a man had just died. But it felt like my future had too. I'd come to England for a new start. But maybe I was being stupid. Maybe I'd let the internet fool me into thinking this was the sort of thing that happened to people when it didn't.

Maybe I should have stayed in New York. I'd been fired a few weeks ago, right before the letter came, alerting me to the inheritance. I'd seen it as a sign from the universe that this was what I was meant for. My company had posted record profits just days before I had been accused of stealing. Which I hadn't done. I was a lot of things, but a thief wasn't one of them. But New York was an at-will state, and I found out from a former co-worker a few weeks later that I'd been replaced by the daughter of the CFO. It figured. But maybe I should have stuck to my original plan. Found a new job. Climbed the corporate ladder. Worked myself to the bone to be successful so that I could buy a nice place, win awards, and have the respect of my peers. Maybe it was stupid to think that in a whole new country, I might feel a bit different. That I might connect with something in a way that felt more than superficial.

I pulled myself away from the depressing spiral of thoughts running through my head. This wasn't forever. The body would be moved, and I could still run this place if people were willing to come in. The ceilings in this store were high; at least fifteen feet. The exposed beams that ran along the ceiling were gorgeous and obviously original, though the ceiling had been painted a gross dark brown to match. The windows at the front let in a lot of natural light, even through the newspapers that covered them, but the shelves Carl had bought were all huge. Most of them were at least eight feet tall, which blocked out most of the light and gave the whole place a real claustrophobic feel. I walked between the shelves, half of which were empty.

Honestly, this place was kind of depressing.

At the back of the store was a glossy black counter. On it sat a computer that looked old enough to run Windows 95 and piles of paper so tall they'd have been an archaeologist's wet dream.

I turned and checked out the books on the shelves. Sure enough, what Maggie and Sophie had said appeared to be right. There were all the latest bestsellers but not much more than that. There were too many shelves for the number of books, too. This space was too big for what Carl had to offer. I knew that straight away. No one wanted to look at a bare shelf. The allure of a bookstore was coming in and being surrounded by books, not by empty shelves.

Plus the books he did carry, he had twenty copies of. No, this was all wrong. All completely wrong. I knew exactly what I'd be doing to this place. I just hoped I'd have the opportunity to fix it.

As if right on cue, a moment later, the front door opened, and I walked back to the entrance to find a man standing there. He was around five foot seven, and his round face was even redder than the thin patch of hair on top of his head. His expression was dour, and his eyes immediately turned to me.

"Maggie, who is this?" he asked.

"My granddaughter, Mackenzie."

"You don't have a granddaughter."

"I do now, obviously, or I wouldn't have said it." Maggie clearly wasn't taking any guff from this guy. "But given as she's alive and well, as you can see, perhaps your energy would be better spent looking at Greg, who's not."

"Who found the body?"

"I did," I said.

"And why were you here?"

"Because this store is mine now. I inherited it from my father, Carl Summers, and I came to see what it looked like."

The man narrowed his eyes at me. "Your father?"

"Yes."

"And who are you?"

"Mackenzie Owens. Who are you?"

"Sergeant Oliver Peters, Devon and Cornwall Police. When did you arrive on the scene?"

"Maybe ten minutes ago."

"Did you touch the body?"

"Only to check for a pulse."

"Do you know him?"

I shook my head. "No."

"When did you arrive in England? I haven't seen you in town."

"Yesterday morning."

"Did you know Greg at all?"

"Nope."

"Did you kill him?"

"Oh, come on," Maggie interrupted. "Are you serious? She just told you she's been in the country for less than twenty-four hours. You don't even know when the time of death was."

Sergeant Peters turned to my grandmother. "Did *you* kill him?"

"Now you're just insulting me. Do you really think that if I was going to murder Greg, I would do so on the floor of the shop my son owned? No. Of course I didn't kill him. If I had, you'd never have found the body."

"Is that your defense? That you wouldn't have been caught if you'd killed Greg?"

"You're bloody right it is. And if you'd like to prove otherwise, I recommend you try finding some actual evidence rather than accusing the people who called you to alert you of this crime of having committed it."

"Fine. Get out of here for now. I need to call a, uh, a crime scene team in. This has never happened before under my watch."

"That's more good luck than good measure," Maggie replied.

"What's that supposed to mean?"

"Nothing at all," Maggie said, plastering a fake smile on her face. "Now, I need a cuppa. Mackenzie and I will be at the Ugly Mug if you need us."

"Have I told you you're free to leave?" Sergeant Peters asked?

"No, but you never told that thin patch on top of your head you call hair to take a hike, and yet it did."

I covered up my laugh with a cough, and Sergeant Peters's face went redder than my cousin Nicky's face when he ate a whole chili pepper on a dare at a party.

I went to grab my coffee and cheesecake from the shelf, but Peters interrupted with a commanding, "Leave that."

I turned and raised an eyebrow. "This is mine. I brought it in with me, and set it down so I could see if the man on the floor was dead. It's not evidence."

"I can't be sure of that," Peters replied. "Everything in here stays in here. Go get yourself another slice of cake if you really need it."

"Are you serious? You're commandeering the best-looking slice of cheesecake I've ever seen? If you want a coffee and donut, just ask."

"If you continue to argue with me, I'll have to consider that to be harassment of an officer."

I briefly considered picking the cake up out of the box and hurling at him. At least then I'd vaguely deserve the charge. And he would have deserved a slice of cake to the face.

But, I decided against it. The cheesecake didn't deserve that fate.

"I want it logged into evidence, and I want it back, or I want to be compensated for it with another slice," I said, as Maggie pulled me from the building and back out onto the street.

I breathed in the salt-tinged air, looking out at the beach and the turquoise waters in front of us. I blinked hard, trying to make sure all of this was real. In the sky above, the gulls had woken up, their cries melting into the light breeze. I followed Maggie back to the Ugly Mug.

Sophie greeted me with a grin. "Back already, babes? And you've come with Maggie."

"Unfortunately, it's because I've been kicked out of the bookstore," I said. "And worse, the police took my cheesecake. Do you know Greg Hamlisch?"

"Sure. Local deadbeat. The boss had to ban him from this place. He kept making shady business deals in here over coffee, and Albert was worried it would draw in a seedier crowd, so he banned him for good. Don't tell me you've already run into him."

"Well, you could say that. He's dead and lying in the middle of the bookshop," Maggie said.

Sophie blinked a couple of times, her brow furrowing as if she hadn't heard right. "Excuse me? Could you repeat that?"

"Greg's dead. Murdered. Someone stabbed him in the bookshop."

"No kidding," Sophie murmured. "Well, between that and Mack's arrival in town, there will be no lacking for gossip in here today. Okay, the two of you have a seat, and I'll bring you out something to make you feel better. That had to have been a shock. I wonder who would have killed him."

"That's not going to be a short list," Maggie said wryly.

"No, I guess not."

I thanked Sophie, and Maggie and I headed to a table in the corner, away from the couple of other customers who were now seated.

"You do know what this means, don't you?" Maggie said. "Sergeant Peters is obviously rubbing those two brain cells of his together as hard as he can, really trying to light a fire with that friction, and he's going to come to the conclusion that one of us killed Greg."

I nodded. "Yeah. I kind of figured that. Which means we only have one option here: as much as this option horrifies me, we have to work together and find the real killer. Or we're going to be drinking toilet wine."

This wasn't exactly the inheritance I'd expected.

Chapter 5

"I CAN'T BELIEVE THIS," MAGGIE SAID. "I'M stuck finding a murderer with a millennial."

"Oh, please, you think this sucks for *you*? What are you going to do if we have to run away from someone? Complain about your bad knee and hope for mercy?"

"Like you'd do anything other than leave me behind and run for your own life," Maggie snapped at me.

"That's right, I would, because right now, you haven't really given me many reasons to go back for you if it comes down to that. And you complain about me being a millennial, but I'm actually going to be useful here. I know how to use the internet. I don't open up Excel to try and send an email."

"Neither do I. You might think I'm useless, but I don't rely on technology for every aspect of my life. It's a useful tool, but I don't need Google to tell me how to make a cup of tea. I know everyone in this town, whereas you're an outsider. Why would anyone tell you anything? They won't. Especially the older generation. Without me, you'd be dead in the water. You're brand new here. Who do you think would help you?"

The two of us stared each other down. "Fine," I finally said. "The thing is, neither one of us is going to manage this without the other. I can do all the work we need online and the physical stuff."

"Are you calling me weak?"

"I'm calling you old."

"Don't think I'm going to forget that."

"You're literally my grandmother. By *definition*, that makes you old."

"Wrong. You're only as old as you feel. And yesterday, I just about took you out, so don't you go on about how I'm this decrepit old lady. But let's say, for the sake of argument, that you're right and that there are going to be some things that will be better suited to your skill set."

"So, we can move on from this argument and work together, then? Tell me about Greg," I said. "If we're going to catch the killer, I need to know everything about him."

"He's a low-grade scammer, always has been. Has lived his whole life in this area. Generally, Cornwall is a pretty low crime area despite what you've just seen, but we've got our corners of it all the same. Do you know who St. Albinus was, the namesake of this little town?"

I shook my head.

"He was a sixth-century French abbot and bishop who used to pay ransoms when members of his flock were kidnapped by pirates while they trawled along the Loire. Being located where we are, pirates have always been an issue here. Nowadays, of course, they're less about pillaging and plundering and more about smuggling."

"Who knew this cute little seaside town had such a shady underside?"

"It's been there for centuries, and Greg Hamlisch has always had his fingers in the less savory pies. Back when he was young, he was very heavily into those MLM schemes. There was a scheme in Ireland back in the eighties called Irish Liberty. Greg tried something similar here, but luckily for everyone involved, he wasn't very good at it, and he was stopped before too many people lost more than a few hundred quid. He was always a bottom feeder. Never good enough to make enough money to attract too much attention. Always just sneaky enough to get by but not so obvious that he'd get sent to prison and be made an example of."

"What was he into recently, do you know?"

At that moment, Sophie arrived with a cup of tea for Maggie, another iced caramel latte for me, and a plate with some cookies.

"I do," Sophie said, putting the items she

carried down and glancing toward the front counter to make sure there weren't any customers waiting on her. "Or at least, I've heard rumors. Apparently, Greg has been picking up deliveries of certain items being brought in through fishing trawlers and driving them to London for someone local in exchange for a cut."

"Certain items being?" Maggie asked.

"Drugs, from what I understand. Word is someone in town has a hookup in southern Spain who's picking them up from North Africa and bringing them here. A few of the fishermen go out to sea, collect a small amount, come back to shore with it in their coolers under a few fish, then they pass it off to Greg, who takes it to their man in London. You know, he drives the speed limit. If the coppers pull him over, he's a respectable, middle-aged white man. Not the kind of guy whose car mysteriously has grounds to be searched."

"The things you hear working at the local coffee shop," Maggie muttered. "I joined Miranda's bloody book club a year ago because I thought I'd hear all the good gossip there, but all they want to talk about is prune juice and who's annoying daughter is marrying what twit."

Sophie winked. "If you keep your ears open, a lot gets said here. If you're looking for the killer, that's where I'd start."

"Do you know who he's working for?" I asked. "Who else is involved?"

Sophie shook her head. "Sorry. All I have are those rumors. And I mean, come on, babes, it was Greg. He was bound to be into more than a few sketchy things. Everything the man did was shady. But that's the one thing I've heard of, recently. This drug thing."

"Hold on," I said, holding up a hand. "Before moving here, I did a modicum of research. I know the economy here isn't what it was in the seventies and eighties, what with flights to Europe being cheap these days. But I thought overall, this was a cute little area. And now I'm hearing stuff about drug smuggling and piracy? This isn't exactly what I expected."

Maggie gave me a wry smile. "Not everything is perfect in paradise, is it? No. Of course, when you read information on the internet, it will show off all the great things about St. Albinus. No one wants to run a tourism website that talks about the seedy underbelly of a place. But it's there. You just won't see it if you're a tourist coming over for a week over the summer. To them, this place is idyllic. Gorgeous, surrounded by nature, and full of friendly, welcoming people wanting to make them feel as though this were their second home. But it's like anywhere else, really. There's crime. Not a lot of it compared to other places, but it's there. And in this town, Greg was always at the center of it."

"Okay. Who were his friends?" I asked. "The other shady characters he might have hung around with."

"We'll speak with them later," Maggie said. "Right now, we need to find out about the drug smuggling."

"Great. How are we going to do that?"

"You're the young person. How would you go about getting drugs? We have to find their source."

I gaped at Maggie. "Are you serious? Here in England? I don't know."

"The television always makes it look so simple, doesn't it? You find somebody, and you ask them, and you make a deal."

"Yeah, only you've got to have a contact. I'm not going to walk up to some random and go 'good morning, kind stranger, would you happen to know where I could buy some cocaine around here?' That's a great way to get myself arrested, and fast."

"How do you find the contact, then?"

"Word of mouth. You meet someone who knows someone who knows someone. That's what you said you're good at, right? You know everyone in this town."

"Well, not the drug dealers."

I raised an eyebrow. "But you could meet them."

"And who would believe me? As you said,

I'm old. No one expects someone to decide they want to try coke in their sixties."

"I think you could make them believe it."

Sophie grinned. "I think that's an excellent idea."

"You're an artist, aren't you?" Maggie asked Sophie. "You art people are always into the fancy new drugs. Can you help us?"

"Sorry, the strongest drug I take is ibuprofen," Sophie said with a shrug. "I can't help you."

"You're an artist?" I said, turning to Sophie.

"Not much of one." She grinned. "Not enough drugs, I guess. I have to go—a couple of customers just came in."

Sophie headed back behind the counter, and I turned to Maggie. "All right, so how are we going to do this?"

"Well, Susan Childs has this grandson she's always complaining about. Good-for-nothing twenty-year-old who's living his life in a marijuana haze. If anyone would know from whom I could purchase drugs, it would be him."

"Try not to use the word 'whom' when you're talking to him," I suggested.

Maggie rolled her eyes. "Really?"

"Yes. It's a drug deal, not tea with the queen. You don't want to scare him off. Which, I mean, you're probably going to do anyway. Maybe I should talk to him."

"Not a chance. You're an outsider. I know his grandmother."

"That makes him *way* less likely to sell you drugs. Or give you any information you're after."

"Wrong. Now, come on. Let's get out of here. I know where Susan's son hangs out, and the faster we get to the bottom of this case, the less likely we are to become victims of Sergeant Peters and his two brain cells."

"This is the worst idea ever," I muttered.

"Okay, I was right. This was the worst idea ever. We're not doing this," I said, holding up my hands in surrender when Maggie emerged from her bedroom. "Nope. Nope, nope, nope."

"And what exactly is wrong with this?" Maggie asked.

We had gone straight home from the coffee shop, and Maggie said she needed to change before she could meet with the drug dealer. I thought maybe she would swap out her slacks for a pair of jeans or something. But this? This was something else.

Maggie looked like she'd just walked out of a Vanilla Ice music video, if Vanilla Ice's target market had been septuagenarian white people who lived in cozy tourist hamlets on the British seaside.

Her slacks had been replaced by jeans that were so oversized they surely must have belonged to Carl, because there was no way she'd have owned them herself. She'd made a belt for them out of a piece of rope that had probably been used to hold up a set of blinds in the past. On top, she had on a soccer jersey, a weird purple-and-green one with 'AIA' written in white letters across the front. Over that was a massive gold chain, and on her head was a pair of oversized Ray Bans. She'd finished off the outfit with a baseball cap flipped backward.

"Everything," I replied. "Everything is wrong with that. No one is going to sell drugs to you. You could not possibly look more like an under-cover cop right now."

"I don't look like a cop, I look *cool*," Maggie snapped at me. "I've got it all: the oversized clothes, the football shirt, the gold chain. I look like someone who would buy drugs."

"You look like Keith Richards trying to dress like Eminem for Halloween."

"Well, that's what we're going for, isn't it? Keith Richards has bought a few drugs in his day."

"That's absolutely not what we're going for. No one is going to take you seriously like this, and they're *definitely* not going to sell you drugs. Let alone give you information about who they're working with. This was a bad idea. I should meet with them."

"No. I told you, no one will sell you drugs."

"Well, they're certainly not going to sell any to *you*, either."

"Fine," Maggie snapped. "I guess I'll just go down looking like a regular old person, not like someone who might want to have some fun in life."

"Good," I said, throwing my arms up in frustration. "That's exactly the way we're going to get some answers."

"I still think this outfit is a good idea," Maggie muttered as she turned and headed back up the stairs to her room to change. When she emerged again five minutes later, she was back to being dressed normally. "Kids these days are supposed to be accepting of anything. Men wearing eyeliner and lipstick. Not that I care, mind you. It's better than the mid-two thousands, when a man who showered once a day was considered metrosexual."

I laughed. "I agree there. But that outfit was not a good idea. This is way better. Besides, don't you know this kid? He'll be well aware that the whole Gangster Granny thing wasn't you at all."

"I've only met him once or twice. He's Susan's grandson. She's complained about him a whole lot, though."

"Okay, where's he going to be?"

"According to Susan, he likes to smoke behind the library. There's a small park. Well, more like a cluster of trees. It's out of view of the road, and the less savory types like to commit their mischief there."

"Lead the way. We have ourselves some drug dealers to find."

Chapter 6

MAGGIE AND I LEFT THE HOUSE, AND SHE immediately headed back toward the center of town, with me following after her. Although instead of going along the main stretch by the beach, we stayed a few blocks inland before reaching the building.

When I thought of a library, I imagined the buildings I'd grown up with: made of basic brick, one level, painted a shade that had obviously been put on sale at the hardware store, filled with fluorescent lighting and overworked and underpaid but dedicated employees who well and truly loved books.

This, on the other hand, was like a castle. Two stories tall, made of uneven granite bricks that gave it a very rustic look. Large windows on both levels gave the building a regal look, helped by the turret that stuck out from the second story on the corner. The roof was metal and rusting on the top, but that somehow added to the character of the building.

This was the kind of building one entered to find a veritable treasure trove of books.

"Wow," I said, gazing up at the building. "This is nice."

"The backside far less so," Maggie said, motioning with her head toward an alley on the far side. "You stay here. I'll call you and put you on speaker."

I nodded and dug my earbuds out of my purse, slipping them on just in time for my phone to start ringing. I slid my finger over the screen to answer.

"Can you hear me?" Maggie asked on the other end of the line.

"Loud and clear."

"Good. Listen carefully to everything he says. We never know what might help us find out who the killer is."

There was silence on the other end of the line for about thirty seconds, and then I heard Maggie's voice again.

"Good morning, gentlemen."

I winced inwardly. No one trying to buy coke ever referred to their potential dealers as "gentlemen."

"If the rest of you don't mind, I'd like to speak with Harry here alone for a couple of minutes."

"Why's the old lady coming after you,

mate?" a man's teasing voice on the other end of the line asked.

"Dunno. She's a friend of me grandmother's, I think," another replied. "All right. I got this. Give us a minute, will you?"

"You sure you're gonna be all right?" another man teased, and there came the chuckles of gentle teasing on the other end of the line.

They faded away, and about fifteen seconds later, Harry spoke again. "What do you want, then? Is everything all right with Nan?"

"She's fine. Well, other than the hemorrhoids. And I think I'm the one who came out worse off after that conversation. Your grandmother told me things I'm never going to be able to forget."

"What? Gross. Why are you here, then?"

"I need some coke, and I figured you can get some for me."

I pressed the tips of my fingers into my eyes and tried to breathe calmly. I wanted to scream into the phone that this was not at all the right way to go about this. Maggie should have been way more subtle.

"Like, a fizzy drink?" Harry asked, obviously confused. "You can get those at any shop on the corner. I mean, if you really want to…"

"Not that kind of coke, you nitwit. Cocaine. Blow. Crack. Nose candy. Snow. Dust. Yayo. Whatever you want to call it, I want it."

My eyes widened. Damn. Maggie knew her slang.

"What the hell, Grandma?"

"Who are you calling Grandma?"

"You. You're literally a friend of me nan. What are you doing out here getting coke for? It don't make any sense."

"Do you have access to cocaine or no?"

"Look, I can't just sell this stuff to you. Why do you want it? You're not using. So no. I don't have any. I don't know where you could find any, either."

I rolled my eyes. I knew this had been a bad idea. No kid in their twenties was going to sell coke to a friend of his grandmother's that he'd probably known his entire life. They might not have trusted me, an outsider, but Maggie was being crazy suspicious just by asking.

"All right, tuss, listen here. This is how it's going to go. You're not only going to sell me a bit of cocaine, but you're going to tell me where it comes from. Who's your dealer, what the distribution system looks like. And don't you look at me like that. I know drugs are big business these days. I want to know how it works. You can either tell me what I want to know, and I've got a hundred here for you, or you can call me a crazy old lady and tell me to get lost, and I'll show you just how nuts I can be."

"Oh yeah? How's that?" Harry was trying to

sound tough, but I could just hear a note of fear in his voice.

"You still live at home, don't you? Well, thanks to Susan, I know your mother. Heather, isn't it? Lovely woman. Hopeless parent, the way you turned out, but a sweet thing herself. She thinks the world of me, too. She'd invite me in for a cup of tea any day of the week. Do you know how easy it would be for me to plant pornography in your room, Harry? And I don't mean *Playboy*. I'm talking deranged. Hentai, from Japan. Do you know what that is? Manga tentacle porn. Imagine what your poor mother would think if she found that in your room. Can you imagine how she'd react?"

"You wouldn't dare," Harry squeaked.

"It probably wouldn't be too long before she kicked you out. After all, what kind of mother wants to look her son in the eye every day knowing he jacks off to tentacle porn? I could leave dozens in there. Make it look like you have an addiction. Real sick stuff."

"I don't! I don't do that!" Harry protested.

"Oh, *I* know that, but your mother doesn't."

"I'll tell her you did it."

"Who do you think she's going to believe? The kindly old woman who's been such a good friend to her mother or her good-for-nothing ratbag of a child who's spending his days hanging out behind the library, selling drugs?"

"You're a crazy old bitch, you know that?"

"You're far from the first person to say that to me. But it doesn't have to be this way, Harry. Your mum doesn't have to believe you're a pervert. All I need is information. And maybe a bit of coke. Five minutes, though, and I'm out of your hair forever. Your hentai secret is safe with me."

"I don't have a hentai secret!" Harry shouted.

"Not if you raise your voice like that, you don't."

"Look," Harry hissed, much more quietly this time.

I stifled a giggle. Okay, I had to hand it to her. Maggie knew what she was doing. She was getting that information.

"Fine. I'll do what you want, okay? Then, you'll leave me alone?"

"Promise."

"What do you want to know?"

"So it's true you deal drugs?"

"Wait, you're not wearing a wire or anything, right? The coppers aren't going to jump out from the trees and arrest me the minute I talk to you?"

"The police? I would rather chop off my right arm than help them with anything. And that's the one I use for—"

"Okay, ew, don't finish that sentence," Harry interrupted quickly. "Why would you say something like that?"

"What? I was going to say peeling potatoes," Maggie replied.

I bit back more laughter. I had to admit, the old lady was growing on me. It turned out that when she wasn't trying to kill me, she was actually kind of funny. And a surprisingly good interrogator, given that she wasn't afraid to threaten to expose a guy's fake porn addiction to his mom.

"I'm not wired up. Greg was killed in my son's shop, and I want to know what he was into. From what I heard, it was drug smuggling."

"Where'd you hear that?"

"It's a small town," Maggie shot back. "Now, you know what's going on. Tell me how it works. Who's your boss?"

Harry sighed on the other end of the line. I had a feeling he was weighing up his options. Eventually, he spoke. "Guy named Dirk. Works out of Penzance. We meet up once a week and do our business. It's not a big thing for me. Just on the side, you know? I got a real job too. This pays better than checking out groceries, though."

"I bet."

"But I don't want any trouble, you know what I mean? I get in, I do my business, and I get out."

"This Dirk, he'd be more into it, though, wouldn't he? Smuggling?"

"Yeah. Me, I'm a small player in his game.

His big thing is moving drugs into the cities. London, Birmingham, Manchester, Liverpool. All the big markets. Running the county lines. He offered me a job once, extra pay if I could take a suitcase up to Newcastle for him. Told him no way. Far too risky. They have those dogs that sniff out drugs these days and stuff. I'm okay with dealing a bit for some extra cash on the down-low, you know, but the stuff he was talking about, that's big money, but it's bigger risk. I'm no idiot."

"Do you know who Dirk did get to move the drugs for him?"

"Not a clue. Was Greg one of them, then? Sounds like the sort of thing he'd be into."

"It does, doesn't it? How much was Dirk going to pay you?"

"Ten grand for that first trip. Said if I managed it successfully, there'd be more where that came from. But he wanted me to tidy up a bit first. Said I had to look like I had a proper job in the City. Suit and tie, that sort of thing. Make me look less suspicious. But I still said no. Wasn't worth it to me."

"Ten grand is a lot of money."

"Can't spend shit if you're in jail."

"I'm impressed. You probably did, in fact, make the right decision. But what's going to stop you getting arrested here?"

"Look, as long as I keep what I'm doing on the down-low, no one knows. The cops aren't aware. I have a small list of clients, and they know it's in their best interest to keep their mouth shut about me. I'm careful, too. I won't say more than that."

"All right. Where can I find Dirk? And what's his last name?"

"Dirk Evers. Comes into town once a week, on Wednesdays. Likes to have lunch at the Horny Goat."

The Horny Goat? Who names a pub that?

"He'll be there today, then?"

"Yeah. Short guy. Dark hair. Beard. Wears thick, red-framed glasses. You won't be able to miss him."

"Thank you for your help, Harry."

"You're not going to… you know, do anything, right? With the magazines? And me mum?"

"No, I'm not. You've been very helpful."

"I still don't get why an old lady like you wants to know all this stuff about drug dealing and Greg's killer. Don't you have, like, a knitting class to get to?"

"Assumptions about the elderly are a dangerous thing, Harry. I might be old, but I'm not in the ground just yet. I have my reasons. Now, I'm sure we'll both be happier pretending this conversation never happened."

"You got that right."

There was silence on the other end of the

line for a moment, then I heard Maggie's voice. "You got all that, Mack?"

"Loud and clear," I replied as she emerged from the alley. I ended the call and pulled the earbuds from my ears as Maggie moseyed across the street. I'd never thought of people her age as being spry and athletic; my other grandmother had been the kind of woman who believed sports were for men, and she had already used a cane in her fifties.

"We got ourselves a name. Although you heard how much grief he gave me. You should have let me wear the outfit."

"That would have scared him even more."

"True, and he was one little explicit threat away from making his own mud puddle already. And we got a name. And a description."

"Yeah. Plus, if he's a regular at the pub, I'm betting people working there are going to know him too. By the way, is it really called the Horny Goat?

"Sure is," Maggie replied with a grin.

"I need to know the story behind that one."

"Oh, believe me, you don't want to. Now, come on. It's nearly eleven. They'll be opening for lunch soon. Let's see what we can uncover."

Chapter 7

THE HORNY GOAT WAS A COZY LITTLE PUB, located on the far end of Wharf Street, in a stone building with an old-fashioned sign hanging from the front. The script, in cursive letters, was surrounded by a rather cartoonish depiction of a goat on its hind legs with a lewd expression on its face, holding a cigar in one hoof. In red, below, were the words "Established 1872".

It was not the classiest image I'd ever seen. We entered through the front doors to find ourselves inside a low-ceilinged pub. The back wall was a bar made of dark mahogany, with every spirit under the sun on the shelves behind it. Against the other three walls were booths upholstered in dark green, and the center was taken up with plain, black wooden chairs and round tables haphazardly spread about.

An acrid smell lingered, and it took me a

second to place it: over a hundred years of cigarette smoke so engrained in the wood that it was now part of the atmosphere despite smoking no longer being permitted indoors.

Behind the bar, a chubby man with a round, red face wiped down the counter with a rag that looked like it was doing more harm than good. A woman about my age with black hair that stuck out in every direction, apart from a streak of bright red in her bangs, nudged the swinging door to the kitchen with her hip as she carried a large tray laden with dirty plates.

A handful of customers eyed us as we came in. The crowd here looked pretty rough; this was definitely a local hangout rather than a tourist haven for families on vacation.

"Maggie," the man called out. "Haven't seen you in here in ages."

Maggie walked up to the counter, and I followed her. We settled in on a couple of stools.

The man leaned in toward us. "I hear there's been a spot of trouble up at the bookshop. I am sorry to hear that, Maggie. It can't be easy, so soon after losing Carl."

"Thank you, Dave," Maggie replied. "It's been difficult for sure. Although I have got a new granddaughter out of it. This is Mack; she was Carl's little secret."

Dave raised his eyebrows as he looked at me. "Carl had that kind of secret, you say? Wouldn't have picked him as the type."

"Neither would I, but she's legitimate. She'll be taking over the bookshop once all this nonsense about a body is over. Assuming Peters doesn't throw her in jail, the moron."

"You've heard me say all cops are bastards a few times in my day, but in Peters's case, they need an addendum: that cop's an idiot as well as a bastard." Dave turned to me. "So you're going to take over that bookshop, you say? The property has promise. If you do it right, I reckon you could make a decent living out of it."

"Well, first, we need to figure out who killed Greg in the middle of the floor in it, and we've been told one of your regulars might have had something to with it. Dirk Evers."

Dave considered Maggie's words for a second then nodded. "Ah, yes. Know the name, know the man. He's a regular, all right, though what I know about his business I couldn't quite say."

"Oh, don't be shy, Dave. You so rarely are," Maggie said.

"Look, I don't want any trouble. Peters is an idiot, but he's an idiot with a badge, and I don't want to draw him into a place like this just because Dirk Evers happens to be one of my customers. I have other customers here who would be made rather nervous by a police presence."

"Well, you should have told Greg not to get himself murdered. I have news for you, Dave:

the police are coming whether you want them to or not. I don't care what you tell them, but you want to talk to us. Tell us about Dirk."

Dave glanced around the room as if trying to make sure no one was going to listen in on the conversation. He leaned forward conspiratorially. "Look, I don't know anything for sure, okay? But given the way people were coming and going when Dirk would come in here to have lunch, I don't think he was on the up-and-up, if you know what I mean."

"You must have some details."

"I don't, and I mean it. He sat at a booth, never at the bar. Wait for Christine to get back; she might know more. He'd chat to her sometimes when she brought him his food."

"What about Greg?" I asked. "You must have known him."

"Aye, certainly did. Now, the fact he's been murdered, that one's not going to come as a surprise to most in this town. I remember back in the nineties, one of his earliest scams. Tried to sell me a property that he didn't quite have the rights to. Luckily, if I know one thing, it's to always pay for a good solicitor. She got to the bottom of things before the money changed hands. Of course, Greg apologized profusely when I called him out on it. Said it was all just a big misunderstanding. He was just a young man trying to make it in this world. Well, he was young at the time, anyway."

"Did you go after him? Legally, I mean?" I asked.

"Nah. Back in the nineties, my heart was softer and my belly harder. It's a bit the other way around now, but Greg didn't have the same reputation back then. I thought he might have just been an honest bugger trying to make a living who'd made a genuine mistake, so I let it slide. After all, no harm no foul, right? And he really did seem so genuine when he apologized. Paid my solicitor's fees, too. That was all I wanted. But that's the kind of person Greg was. He had charisma."

Maggie nodded. "That's why people trusted him."

"Exactly right. People like that, they make people like them. They draw them in, they say all the right things, and then they strike."

"Do you know anyone else who's had issues with Greg recently?" Maggie asked.

Dave glanced away, obviously hiding something.

"Oh, come off it. Someone murdered him, Dave. Shoved a knife in his chest and left him to bleed out on the floor of my son's shop. You really want someone who's able to do that walking around free in this town? We have to be able to sleep at night too, you know."

Dave sighed, taking the rag he'd been using and throwing it into a trash can against the wall behind him. "Fine. You're right. I just hope it wasn't someone local who did this to him. But Greg was the kind of guy who didn't mind shitting where he ate. He ruined a few lives here, those of people who didn't know better."

"Anyone recent?"

"Aye, Johnny Williams. You know him, I assume."

"Certainly do," Maggie replied with a nod. "Manager at the bank, isn't he? New to the job. Down here from London or Manchester or somewhere like that."

"That's the one. Poor lad came in with bright eyes and a master's degree from one of them fancy universities up there and got a quick lesson in how the real world works. Felt bad for the bloke, but what can you do? Word is, he had to call up his bosses and explain the whole thing. Got reamed out real badly. He came in here to drown his sorrows, told me all about it. Said he'd never expected something like that to happen in a place like this. He lapped up the tourist brochures about St. Albinus and thought he was coming into a gorgeous destination and would find his whole life to be a holiday. Well, bully for him, it turns out we've got a bit more than just beaches and cute cafés."

"Was he fired?" I asked.

"No. Lucky bugger if you ask me. I'd have thought the suits up in London would have fired him in a minute, but they chalked it up to youthful inexperience and gave him another chance."

"How much did Greg take him for?" Maggie asked.

"Twenty thousand quid from the bank's coffers, I hear. That's not from the horse's mouth, though. Poor Johnny is on thin ice now, and he felt like a right patsy. Which he was. But men have killed over less."

Maggie nodded. "We'll speak to him. Who else?"

"Norman Bally owes him a fair bit of cash over an old gambling scheme. Greg caught him in here a few weeks ago. I was at the bar. Not listening in, of course. Just that their voices happened to carry over to me, if you know what I mean."

"Naturally," Maggie replied.

"Well, Greg was being rather unkind to poor Norman, who, it turns out, had a stroke of bad luck betting on the footy. He's been a Tottenham fan his whole life, so in a way, he shouldn't be that surprised, bad luck is where he lives."

"Ah, the equivalent of a Buffalo Bills fan," I said, nodding in understanding.

"Right, that'd be the team in American football. Well, turns out Norm owed Greg about ten grand. Greg was coming after him to collect, but from what I gather, Norm didn't have the money and had no ETA on when he expected to get it, either. Greg wasn't thrilled about this development and told Norm if he wasn't going to pay, Greg was going to have to make an example out of him. Asked Norm if he wanted to get a really good look at his old man's cricket bat."

I raised my eyebrows. "That's a pretty explicit threat. When was this?"

"Oh, three days ago? Maybe four now. It was recent enough that it's got me wondering if Norm didn't think this was the easiest way to wipe his debt."

I nodded in agreement.

"Here's Christine now," Dave said, motioning for the server to come over as she reemerged from the kitchen carrying another tray full of food. She tilted her head in the direction of one of the tables then dropped off their food before returning behind the bar.

"What's up?" she asked, flashing a smile to me and Maggie.

"You know Maggie, of course, and this is her new granddaughter, Mack."

Christine raised her eyebrows. "Well, between this and Greg being found stabbed in the bookshop this morning, that's going to keep the town chattering for months. How did Carl end up with a new daughter no one knew about, including, I presume, Maggie?"

"This was news to me too," my grandmother confirmed. "Anyway, Carl knew about Mack but never got in touch, left her in the will, and here we are. She'll be taking over the bookshop once the body's been taken away, assuming she's still interested."

"Oh, please, I'm not going to let somebody dying in that building keep me from living out my dream. Although I will say, the news articles and memes about travelling overseas to run a cute little bookstore in a perfect location never mentioned murder."

"That's the spirit," Christine said. "So, what's going on?"

"As it turns out, Sergeant Peters has decided the two of us are the most likely people to have put that knife in Greg, entirely due to the fact that we own the property where it happened. Of course, that's not a motive for murder, but Peters isn't going to let a good fact get in the way of him taking the laziest route to a result. Therefore, Mack and I are taking the reins and finding the killer, if only to keep ourselves out of jail."

"Makes sense," Christine said, nodding.

"They're asking about Dirk. I know he comes in here a fair bit, but I've never spoken to him. Seen him chatting to you, though."

Christine's face scrunched into a grimace. "Yeah, if you can call what he was doing chatting. Hitting on me, more like. And not well."

"Did he tell you anything about his business? Or did you ever overhear anything? Especially related to Greg?" Maggie asked.

"Well, I don't know the exact details, but I gather it wasn't especially legal," Christine replied, placing a hand on her hip. "I know he would talk about going out on the water with a mate of his who had a fishing boat, and I had a sneaking suspicion they were moving more than fish, but I couldn't confirm. Greg would come in here and chat with him from time to time, though. I heard them talking about moving product. Shipments to a friend. That sort of thing. Nothing specific, nothing that I could swear was illegal, but knowing both those men, I doubt it was all on the up-and-up."

"What do you suspect?" I asked, pretty sure I already knew the answer.

"Drugs," Christine confirmed. "It had to be drugs around here, surely. But again, I couldn't swear to it. Still, it makes sense. I just didn't want to dig too hard."

It looked as if Harry had been telling us the truth about Greg being into drug smuggling with Dirk.

"Understood," Maggie said. "Thank you for the help. If you don't mind, we're just going to hang out here for a bit to see if Dirk happens to show up. After all, he's either not heard of Greg's death yet, or if he did it, he'll want to make it look like he doesn't know."

"If he doesn't show up, it'll be like playing detective on easy mode," I agreed.

"Can I get you anything while you're waiting?" Christine asked.

"What's good here?" I asked Maggie.

"We'll take two bowls of beef stew," she replied.

"Not going to initiate the newbie with some stargazy pie?" Christine asked, shooting a wink in my direction.

"I haven't ruled it out, but we'll wait until after we've solved this murder."

"What's stargazy pie?" I asked when Christine left.

"Oh, nothing," Maggie replied.

I pulled out my phone. "You do realize it's the twenty-first century and I am an adult with a phone near me at all times that connects to the internet? An internet that gives me access to all of the collective information mankind has ever discovered. And also way too much weird porn. But right now, the endless information is the important part."

I typed "stargazy pie" into Google, and my eyes widened. "Are those… fish heads… sticking out of the pie?"

"Technically, the fish are whole," Maggie said. It's only the fronts of them that stick out. Get it? Stargazy pie? They're looking up, gazing at the stars."

"You could have offered me any amount of money, and I never would have guessed that's what this looked like," I said, closing the tab. "Anyway, I regret looking. The internet was a mistake."

"It's a delicacy in these parts, although I

can't say I blame you if you haven't grown up with it. It's an acquired taste. Lovely but local. You might be a bigger fan of a Cornish pasty. The bakery down the street do one that will make you want to jump down into the mines."

I laughed. "I'm not sure that's a selling point."

"Frankly, the only deal-breaker is if you put the cream on your scones before the jam," Maggie said. "If that's how you live, I'm going to have to disown you as my grandchild."

"I've never had especially strong opinions about scones."

"Oh, you better have one if you want to live here."

"Don't look now, but your man just walked in," Dave said quietly without so much as glancing at the front door. "I'll tell the kitchen to make that stew up to go, will I?"

"Lovely. Thank you very much," Maggie said.

We waited about a minute or so to let Dirk get settled then got off our stools and walked toward the booth he'd settled in. We already knew he was a drug dealer. But there was a good chance I was also staring at the man who had plunged a knife into Greg's heart.

Chapter 8

Dɪʀᴋ Eᴠᴇʀs ᴡᴀs ᴛʜᴇ ᴋɪɴᴅ ᴏꜰ ɢᴜʏ ᴡʜᴏ ᴜsᴇᴅ too much gel in his hair, whose smile was a little bit too white, and who showed just a few too many teeth when he flashed it at you. He was dressed casually, in faded jeans and a light sweater, but looking at him, I got the impression that he still spent twenty minutes staring at his closet and carefully picking out exactly what clothes would give the impression he wanted to convey today.

He gave off alien vibes, as if he was the kind of psychopath who had to spend time trying to figure out what the humans would expect him to wear in order to blend in properly.

I had known quite a few people like that when I worked in a corporate office. The disappointing part was that they tended to be loaded.

Dirk casually perused the menu as Maggie slipped into the booth across from him, and I immediately joined her. He looked up at us, surprise registering in his expression for just a moment, disturbing the mask of politeness that almost instantly went up again.

"Well, good morning to you lovely young ladies," he said. "To what do I owe this pleasant visit?"

"Greg Hamlisch," Maggie replied. "We hear you know him."

"We're certainly acquainted."

"Are you acquainted with the knife that was jammed into his chest? Did you put it there?" Maggie asked.

Dirk tilted his head to the side slightly. "I'm sorry?"

"Murder, Dirk. Greg was murdered. Did you do it?"

This time, the veneer of politeness fell from Dirk's face and didn't return. "Someone killed Greg? Are you serious?"

"You're welcome to go down to the bookshop and have a look for yourself if you don't believe me. I'm sure the police have the whole place cordoned off right now. Or are you faking because you're the one who killed him?"

Dirk ran a hand down his face. "You're joking. You must be joking."

"We'd have to be psychopaths to think this was funny," I replied.

"This is bad. Awful."

"It is. And it's going to get a lot worse for you if you don't talk to us," Maggie said.

"I have to make some calls," Dirk replied almost as if he didn't hear us.

"Not before you speak to us," I replied.

Dirk paused, his eyes going from one of us to the other. "No offense, ladies, but right now, I have bigger things to deal with than you."

"That's because you don't realize what a nightmare we're going to be for you if you don't listen to us," Maggie said, the polite, old-lady smile never leaving her face. "Because here's what we know: you're a drug runner. You do the main handoff out in the water, far from shore, where there's no one to catch you. Maybe you cover your goods with fish to deter any authorities from taking a close look. Then, when you're back on shore, you work with a network of people to move the goods into different parts of the country.

"Greg was one of these men for you, wasn't he? He moved the drugs for you. And while I'm not really the kind of person that's normally inclined to help the police with their investigations, if you get out of that booth before we're finished with you, I'm going to make an exception."

Dirk paused, staring at Maggie as if disbelieving that she'd just said those words to him. "What?"

"You heard me, and I will not be repeating

myself. We have some questions to ask you. Whatever you have to organize can wait unless you want the police banging down your door and asking questions you really don't want to have answered. After all, we've figured this all out, and we're just a local old lady and a woman who's lived in town less than twenty-four hours. How long do you think it's going to take the police, with all their resources, if they really put their minds to it?"

Realizing he had no other options, Dirk slumped back down in his seat, and I bit back a smile. Maggie was good at this. "Fine. Okay. What do you want to know?"

"First of all, you still haven't answered my question: did you kill Greg?" Maggie asked.

"What? No, of course I didn't. I didn't know he was dead. This is really going to mess things up for me."

"Yes, truly, *you* have had a bad day," I deadpanned.

"Look, Greg was a decent guy, but it was all business between us. And if you tell anyone about any of this, I'll deny it all."

"Who's going to believe an old lady and an outsider?" Maggie replied. "We're not going anywhere with this information. We're just trying to find the killer. So, Greg moved the drugs for you. To London?"

Dirk nodded. "Yeah. He was the perfect guy for it too. You know who's the best? Women and middle-aged white men. The police never suspect them of anything, even when they get pulled over. It's all 'oh, your taillight is out, get that replaced as soon as possible' or 'were you aware you were doing ten over the limit?' but that's it. Greg was perfect."

"How long did he do this work for you?"

"Six months. One shipment a month. I have some other business I run out of town here, and I come by once a week. Whenever Greg was done with a shipment, he would meet me here. I'd pass him his pay under the table, he'd be on his merry way a couple minutes later, and that was that."

"Any problems with him? Did you know if Greg had any issues?"

"We weren't friends. Things between us were strictly business. When he came in, we'd exchange pleasantries, and he'd be on his way not five minutes later. I don't know much of anything about him."

"How did you initially make contact, then?" I asked. "How could you bring him on board if you didn't know him?"

"A friend of mine that I trust very much recommended that I speak with Greg and that the two of us would be able to work together in a way that would be mutually beneficial."

"Who is that friend?" Maggie asked.

"I'm afraid I'm not at liberty to say," Dirk replied.

"You're not going to be at liberty at all if you don't tell us what we want to know," I replied. Out of the corner of my eye, I saw Maggie nodding slightly in approval.

Dirk glanced around as if looking for an exit strategy that would get him out of this conversation faster. But none was forthcoming.

"It's really not that hard, Dirk," I said. "You can tell us what we need to know. We then leave you alone and speak to this mutual friend. Your name doesn't need to come up at all. We're just trying to figure out who killed Greg."

"Fine. Jeremy. Jeremy Haggerty. Lives in town here."

"And how about you?" I asked. "Have you been in town the past few days?"

"No," Dirk snapped. "I come here once a week. That's it. I haven't been around. And I didn't kill Greg. Why would I? This complicates my life. He did good work for me. I had no reason to want him dead. None at all. Now, I have to find someone to replace him. Do you know how hard it is to find a reliable drug runner these days?"

"I really don't," I replied.

"It's not easy. They say no one wants to work these days. Well, that doesn't just apply to fast food employees. What with all the increases in policing, even when you offer a good wage, a lot of people don't want to take the risk involved in my business. Money's great, but some people would rather not take the chance of getting on the wrong side of the law. And a lot that do, well, they're no use to me. You think I'm going to get a twenty-year-old punk with tattoos on his face and an orange Nissan from 1992 with a pot sticker on his back bumper to shuttle drugs for me? No. That would be stupid. I need a specific kind of person to do this work, and Greg was that kind of person. And he was good at it. I didn't know he was dead, and I'm in a tough spot, really. I didn't kill him."

"All the same, I suppose there's no one who can account for your whereabouts the last two days in their entirety?" Maggie asked.

"No. A man's got to sleep, doesn't he? But I'm telling you, I had nothing to do with Greg's death. Now, if you don't mind, I really do have a number of calls to make. This is really going to mess with my business."

"We just need Jeremy's number," I said.

Dirk pulled out his phone and scribbled out a number on a napkin, sliding it across the table to Maggie. "Don't tell him where you got it."

"We'll be discreet," Maggie said. "Do you happen to have Greg's home address, by the way?"

"Sure. I've had to stop by his place before for business, once or twice." Dirk grabbed the napkin back and jotted down an address underneath Jeremy's phone number.

"Thank you," Maggie said. "You've been very helpful."

"Yeah, well, don't go spreading news of that around, and you'll be doing me a favor."

Taking my cue, I left the booth. At the front counter, Dave had a couple of take-out containers ready to go in a plastic bag.

"Get what you needed?" he asked as Maggie handed him a few bills.

"Hopefully a few more leads, though I don't think Dirk's the killer."

"I suppose it's good news I haven't lost a regular customer, then," Dave said with a wink. "All righty, then, I'll see you around, I'm sure. Nice to meet you, Mack."

"You too," I replied as the two of us headed back out into the street.

"So, what happens now?" I asked.

"First things first, we head home, and we eat this stew. I don't care if Westminster Abbey has caught on fire. Nothing's going to get between me and a good meal."

"Well, I guess that's genetic," I replied as the aroma wafted toward my nostrils and got my mouth watering.

We headed back home, where Maggie ladled out the contents of the container into a bowl and a plate. I soon found myself facing a hearty beef stew with a large chunk of crispy sourdough bread on the side.

"So, what do you think?" I asked as I dug

into the meal. "Dirk doesn't really have any motive to be the killer, does he?"

"Disappointingly, I agree," Maggie replied. "Assuming he's telling us the truth, of course. I wouldn't write him off completely, as you never know. Greg would be the type to decide maybe the money isn't worth the risk he's putting in, and maybe he decided to help himself to a bit of the product and try to sell it on his own. Dirk wouldn't tell us about that."

"No," I admitted.

"You did well making him understand that he had to talk to us," Maggie said, looking at me approvingly. "You have more spunk than I would have expected."

"Oh? Didn't think I'd have it in me?"

"Honestly, no. So far, you've come off as a bit of a whiner. Complaining about how I tried to kill you. That sort of thing. You won't stop talking about it."

I arched a single eyebrow skyward. "It was *yesterday*."

"Yes, my point exactly."

"Okay, well, I'll take the compliment. I guess the next step is talking to Norman Bally? And Jeremy? Do you know where to find Norman?"

"Certainly do. He works as a boat mechanic. Does maintenance for the fleet for one of the tourism companies here in the summer. Then in the winter, he freelances for the fishermen who need it. We'll find him down at the wharf."

"Okay. The thing is, though, I don't like how we're just chasing story after story," I said, tearing off a chunk of bread and using it to spoon up a hefty serving of stew. I chewed and swallowed then continued. "We need to go right to the source. Someone like Greg, we're already finding out that he was involved in illegal activity, and going by what I've learned about him, I don't think we've even scratched the surface of what he was into. And that's already drug running and being a bookie. We need more."

"What are you suggesting?"

"We need to break into Greg's home. That shouldn't be an issue for you. After all, you did try and murder me yesterday, remember?" I added with a grin.

Maggie narrowed her eyes at me, but the corners of her mouth curled up into a smile. "You know, I never thought having a grandchild that reminded me so much of me would be annoying. And yet here we are."

"You're coming off as a bit of a whiner. Does that mean you agree with me?"

Maggie ignored the jab. "I do. I think you're right. We'll wait until tonight. The police won't stay there after five o'clock. Besides, I imagine they'd be finished searching anyway."

"And they won't have surveillance on the property?" I asked.

Maggie snorted. "There might be a seedy underside to this town most holidaymakers don't see, but the police presence isn't big enough to justify it. Up until about ten years ago, if you had a police issue after eight o'clock at night, you had to wait for someone to come by from St. Ives down the road. No, if we wait until the middle of the night, there won't be anyone there to catch us."

I was going to have been in England for less than forty-eight hours before committing my first felony.

Chapter 9

MAGGIE AND I ATE IN SILENCE FOR A LITTLE while.

"So... what was your son like? My dad, I mean," I finally asked. "You haven't talked about him much. It must be hard."

Maggie looked up from her bowl of stew. "It is. I've been quiet about it, because I know you didn't know him. I don't know how interested you are in his life. I wouldn't really blame you if you didn't care. After all, it's not like he was there for you, and he should have been."

I shrugged. "I didn't care before. Not really. But I mean, he was my dad, I guess? Like it or not, I've got half his DNA. And I never thought there was a point in caring before. There wouldn't be anyone to answer the questions, so why bother having them? They'd only lead to disappointment. But now, here we are."

"Here we are indeed."

"He's the link between us. So, what was he like?"

Maggie paused before answering, her eyes glazing over as she thought about what to say. "Carl was a free spirit as a boy. He would run in the fields and the woods. He could name all the birds in the trees and identify most of them by their sounds. And that was where he went. Most of his friends, they liked playing football, all liked to pretend they were Ian Rush. But not Carl. He was more in the clouds than that."

"He was a dreamer."

"Oh, yes. Without question. Carl was the kind of man who thought he would live a life of adventure. He never grew out of that idea. Even as an adult. It's why he moved back here, I think. Cornwall held a kind of romanticism that he couldn't find in London. Even the idea of opening the bookshop was supposed to be this romantic dream he had. But that was Carl. He would expunge his responsibilities in favor of following whatever whim his heart took him to next. That's how you ended up being born without having a father in your life."

I poked at the stew in my bowl. "I guess without his dreaming, I wouldn't be here."

"That is true. Although you also wouldn't be a murder suspect, either."

As if right on cue, there came a knock at the door. Maggie got up and answered it. A moment later, she returned with Sergeant Peters hot on her heels.

Behind him was another man. This man was younger, in his early, maybe mid-thirties. He stood over six feet tall, with three days' worth of dark stubble that couldn't hide a chiseled jaw. His mouth was firm and his black eyes deep set.

"He would like to talk to us," she said simply.

"The forensics unit has completed their investigation at the scene," Sergeant Peters said, eyeing my bowl of stew as if he hadn't eaten for a week. "The pathologist believes the time of death to have been between midnight and four o'clock last night. You were in the country at the time, is that correct?"

"Yes," I replied, crossing my arms in front of me.

Sergeant Peters waited as if he wanted me to say more, but I wasn't about to do that. I knew how the cops worked. I wasn't talking if I didn't have to.

"Did you kill Greg?" the man behind Sergeant Peters asked me.

I looked at him carefully. "Who are you?"

"I'm the one asking the questions here," he replied.

I shrugged and turned back to my stew, picking up my spoon and taking a bite.

"Hey, I asked you a question," the man snapped at me.

"So? Why should I answer it?"

"This is Inspector Jason Hart, brought in from Plymouth to help with the investigation," Sergeant Peters said.

"It must be bad if you've requested help from Devon," Maggie muttered.

"As you are well aware, Devon and Cornwall share a police force. Inspector Hart is an experienced investigator who has looked into similar cases before, and I thought his experience would come in handy in this case," Sergeant Peters said, his nose scrunching up as if he smelled something unpleasant.

"Well, he can't be that good if he's just going to ask me the same thing you did this morning," I said.

"I prefer to hear my answers from the potential witnesses themselves."

"I didn't witness anything."

"Did you kill Gregory Hamlisch?" Inspector Hart asked again.

"Nope."

"Do you know who might have done it?"

"No."

"And you?" Inspector Hart asked, turning to Maggie.

"Wasn't me, either. You're looking in the wrong spot."

"You found the body?" Inspector Hart asked, turning to me once more.

"That's right."

"And you say you didn't know Gregory Hamlisch?"

"Also correct."

"Do you know what he might have been doing in a shop co-owned by the two of you?"

I rolled my eyes. "No. Did you skip over the whole I-didn't-know-him part?"

"I don't skip over anything."

"Yeah, nothing gets by you," I said sarcastically.

"We can continue this conversation at the police station if you'd prefer," Inspector Hart snapped. I had obviously touched a nerve.

"Is that a request for a voluntary police interview?" Maggie asked, her eyes narrowing.

"It certainly is," Inspector Hart replied.

"In that case, not only do we need that request in writing, but the both of us require to have solicitors present. Which means this conversation is over, and if you think you're going to railroad my granddaughter because she's new to the country and doesn't understand the minutiae of our laws, you're very much mistaken."

"You seem to have a lot of knowledge about how the law works," Inspector Hart said, turning to Maggie.

"At least one of us does. And that's because I'm well aware that the police know the laws, and they depend on an uneducated populace who doesn't try to railroad innocent people into being arrested and convicted of crimes they didn't commit. That isn't going to happen here, and I will not allow you to do it to my grand-daughter. If you do arrest her, my first call will be to the American Embassy in London, and my second call will be to *The Guardian*."

Inspector Hart shared a look with Sergeant Peters then turned back to us, the expression on his face having hardened. "All right. This conversation is over for now, and we may send a letter requesting your presence at the station in the future."

"So you're finished messing with my book-store?" I asked. "I can go back there?"

"Yes," Inspector Hart replied.

Without another word, he turned and left, with Sergeant Peters following him.

"You still owe me a slice of cheesecake," I called out after them. When they left, I faced Maggie and raised my eyebrows. "Looks like things are getting serious."

"The only thing worse than one dumb cop is two dumb cops," she replied, pressing her lips together as she glared in the direction the two men had just gone. "We'd better hope we find something tonight, because I wouldn't be surprised if at least one of us is arrested within the week."

"And here I thought uprooting my entire life on a whim was going to be a fun adventure," I muttered. "I'm going to go check out the bookshop this afternoon. You never know; maybe the police missed something. And regardless, we're going to figure this out, and I'm going to run this bookstore. Which means I need to get in there, see what I can do, and figure out how to make it viable."

"The location is excellent," Maggie said.

"It is," I agreed. "And by all accounts, the problem is Carl tried to make it look like every other version of whatever your Barnes and Noble is in the UK."

"Waterstones. You should probably know that if you intend to run a bookshop here," Maggie said.

"Okay, yes. All the bestsellers. But people who come to Cornwall aren't looking for the same thing they can buy at any old store in London. They're looking for something a little bit more curated. Something that doesn't just satisfy everyone but will definitely satisfy them."

"Precisely," Maggie said.

"I'm going to give them that. A bookstore should be more than just a transaction. It should be an experience. That's what's going to make a place profitable, make it stand out, make people want to visit my store. This is what I'm good at. Marketing. Giving people what they want. Making a place that's absolutely perfect. And I get to do it from the ground up," I said. I was excited about this. Running my own bookstore wasn't something I'd ever thought I'd do. I thought I was going to spend my whole life working toward a corner office.

"Going to jail would rather interfere with those plans."

"So that's why we're going to make sure neither one of us ends up in prison over this. But I'm going to head over there soon and start making some changes. I can't let this murder hang over my life while we solve it."

"Good plan," Maggie said.

As soon as I was finished with lunch, I helped to clean the dishes, and before I knew it, I was back on my way toward the bookstore.

This time, when I unlocked the door, I was met with a feeling of unease rather than excitement. After all, the last time I'd done this, I'd come across a dead body. Surely, that couldn't happen twice in one day, though, right? I walked through the entrance, and my gaze immediately fell to the floor where the body had been.

It was gone, now. There was still blood on the floor, though. And black dust everywhere from where the police had gathered fingerprints. I knew it; my coffee and cheesecake were nowhere to be seen.

Many of the books on the shelves had been removed and dumped on the floor, presumably while the police searched for evidence. The computer and point-of-sale system on the counter at the back of the store were gone; rectangles surrounded by dust betrayed where they had been only a few hours ago.

Particles floated through the air, catching in the rays of light that broke through the small gaps in the paper on the windows that blocked the view of the interior of the building from the street.

Right now, this looked like the creepiest place on the planet. But I was going to transform it into something beautiful.

Step one was to get rid of the blood on the floor. I had no idea how I was going to do that, since I wasn't a serial killer.

Okay, I had to make a list. I went back out into the street and reentered the Ugly Mug Café.

Sophie smiled at me when I reached the counter. "Welcome back, babes."

"It's better than being in jail. Any chance you know how to get bloodstains out of a wooden floor? I need to pretend I'm not going to spend the rest of my life rotting away in the Tower of London like a modern-day Anne Boleyn."

"You do realize she was executed, right?"

"Yes, but I can't name anyone else who was held in the tower long term. We don't exactly learn all about English history in American high schools."

"From what I gather, you barely learn about

American history, either," Sophie replied with a grin.

"Well, you're not too far off. But I have to figure out how I'm going to clean the blood. And I think I'm going to need another slice of cheesecake," I continued, eyeing a gorgeous cake that had three slices left. The inside was marbled with vanilla and chocolate.

"Sure. Let me grab you some cake, and I'm going to get Ann to come and help you."

"Ann?"

"She and her husband own this place. I've never seen a woman who can do more with less or a woman who knows how to clean anything better. She'll give you a hand. Hold on."

Sophie pulled out her phone and sent out a quick text then set about packaging up a slice of cheesecake for me. "So, do you know who killed Greg yet?"

I shook my head. "No, but we've got a couple decent leads. It's still early on in the investigation, but I know the police suspect me. I was hoping to take a few hours to clear my head a bit before tonight."

"What happens tonight?"

"Uh, nothing."

"Right, I totally believe you. But you don't have to worry. Ann's on her way, and she'll give you a hand. Here she is now."

"That was quick," I said, raising an eyebrow.

Sophie grinned. "She lives less than a

hundred feet from here. Ann, come and meet Mack."

I turned and found myself facing a tall woman who looked to be in her late fifties. Her blond hair was speckled with gray, plainly cut to her shoulders. She stood at least five foot ten, and on the slimmer side, dressed in a casual pair of slightly oversized jeans and an outdated sweater, with comfortable sneakers on her feet. A pair of glasses hung on a string around her neck, and she immediately came toward me with a warm smile.

"Mack, you must be Carl's secret daughter," she said, reaching out a hand, which I shook.

"That's me," I replied. I supposed that was how everyone in this town was going to know me for a while.

"Mack is going to reopen the bookshop, but there's blood on the floor," Sophie explained. "I told her you know how to get stains out of anything."

If Ann was surprised she was being brought in to help clean a crime scene, she didn't show it. "Of course. Let's just make a quick trip to Wattle's, the DIY shop, and they'll have everything we need."

Sophie handed me my box of cheesecake with a confident smile, and I followed Ann out of the coffee shop.

"You're revamping the bookshop, are you, then?"

I nodded. "I have a lot of ideas for it. I think it could be a really cool space. But of course, people aren't going to want to shop where they can see bloodstains on the floor."

"No. Luckily, the sooner you get into it, the easier it is to get rid of. In the worst case, you might have to get the floors resurfaced where the blood is, but it hasn't been there long, has it?"

"Less than a day."

"Good. I'm sure we'll have you sorted in an hour." She led me through the maze of streets to a small shop tucked away in a corner. A sign above the door announced the name Wattle's, and the interior was filled with stock covering every single inch of the walls, floor to ceiling, to the point where I practically had to walk down the aisles sideways to avoid constantly bumping into anything. But we emerged ten minutes later with our supplies and headed back to the bookstore.

"How's Maggie treating you?" Ann asked as we walked along.

"We got off to a rocky start, but we're getting there," I said.

Ann burst out laughing. "A rocky start, I bet. She's a nutter, that one, but a good egg. I'd recommend staying on her good side if you can."

"That's the goal. I'm not trying to annoy anybody by coming over here."

"Oh, you'll annoy some by sheer virtue of

your arrival, but no one who matters. Some of the people here aren't too keen on outsiders. By which they mean anyone who can't trace their lineage in Cornwall back five hundred years. But don't pay them no mind. It's the twenty-first century. People move, more than they ever have before. You're just as welcome as anyone else planning to live here permanently."

We reached the bookstore, and I opened the front door. I half expected Ann to recoil at the sight of the blood, but instead, she took one glance at it and turned to me. "Have you got a water supply here? This should be a quick and easy fix, not to worry. We'll have you selling books in no time at all."

Thirty minutes later, with the help of lots of water, cloths, dish detergent, steel wool, and a bit of wax, the floor looked good as new. I stood over it and grinned. "Okay, that's the first challenge done."

"What else are you looking to change?" Ann asked.

"I'm going to have to clean up all these piles of books, of course," I said, motioning to the floor, where dozens of discarded tomes lay thanks to the overzealous police. "Then I need to get rid of at least half these shelves. And get smaller ones. This place could feel huge, but right now, the way Carl had it set up, it feels very cramped. It's too dark, too. I need to paint the walls."

Ann nodded. "All very reasonable changes. I can get you the paint. My brother who lives outside of town has a fair bit of extra just lying around."

"Oh, you don't have to," I said automatically.

"I know I don't have to, but I'd like to," Ann replied. "You're a young woman, just moved across the world, trying to make a new life for herself. And if you need any help with construction, give my husband Albert a shout. He's quite skilled, if I may say so myself."

"Thank you so much," I said gratefully. "I thought I was going to have to hire a crime-scene cleaning service or something like that."

"There's no need for that sort of rubbish when I'm around," Ann replied. "I'll be getting back, but if you need anything, you just fire off a quick text, and I'll be here in no time."

Ann left, and I spent the next few hours sorting out books, creating piles, deciding how this place was going to look, and figuring out how I could best live out my dreams of owning a gorgeous store with a budget that was basically in the negatives.

It was going to be fine. I could make this place a success. I knew I could.

By the time the sun began to set and I was getting ready to leave the bookshop, it was nearly nine o'clock at night. I was covered in a thin sheen of sweat, and my muscles ached like I'd just taken part in a strongman competition, but I was slowly organizing this place.

I'd spent a couple of hours online, scouring Facebook Marketplace and Gumtree—what I quickly found out was the UK equivalent to Craigslist—and had come away with a few connections that might lead to some items I needed for the store. And with Ann's husband's help, hopefully, I'd be able to transform some of the shelves in this place and turn it into the cozy, perfect nook I was dreaming of.

But first, it was time to commit a crime in the hopes of proving my innocence of another, worse crime.

Chapter 10

JUST AFTER MIDNIGHT, MAGGIE AND I WERE
ready to go.

"You can't go out dressed like that," Maggie
announced when I came down into the living
room.

"Why not? What's wrong with this? I look
like Catwoman." I had put on a black, long-
sleeved shirt and black tights. My hair was tied
back in a tight ponytail, and I had on a pair of
black ballet flats.

"You look like you're going out to commit a
robbery in the middle of the night," Maggie
replied. "This is St. Albinus. People are going to
be looking out their windows if they hear
anything, and the instant they see you, they're
going to know you're up to no good."

"Oh, yeah, because it's totally normal for
people to be looking out their windows at
midnight. They're not just going to see us

dressed normally and think we're out for a night-time stroll. You especially. I can pretend I'm coming back from the pub or something. But no one your age is out at this hour, ever."

"At least if we're spotting they won't immediately think I'm a criminal."

"No, the best thing to do is to hide in the shadows, so we're not noticed at all. Besides, how many people are going to be up in the middle of the night, looking out their windows just in case a thief happens to be in the area?"

"You'd be surprised," Maggie said ominously.

"Okay. So we've already reached an impasse."

Maggie and I eyed each other. Eventually, she spoke. "Middle ground. Go back up there and dress in something dark but something that doesn't scream 'I'm about to commit a crime. Please call 9-9-9 because I felt the need to play dress-up-like-a-superhero.'"

"Oh, like you can talk; you tried talking to a teenager dressed like an extra from a Vanilla Ice music video," I shot back at her. "But fine."

I went back upstairs and returned a few minutes later. I was still dressed in tights, but I'd changed to my navy-blue sneakers and replaced the skin-tight shirt with a slightly oversized sweater that would still allow me to move freely.

"I suppose that's a bit better," Maggie said when I returned.

"It's all you're getting," I replied. "Now, come on. Let's find out who wanted Greg dead."

We left the house, and I had to admit, as I followed Maggie through the dark streets of St. Albinus, my eyes kept glancing toward the windows, watching for curious locals. But there was nothing. In fact, the town seemed practically deserted this late at night.

Clouds obscured the moon, and as soon as the clock struck midnight all the streetlights suddenly extinguished, plunging the town into pitch black nothingness. Luckily, Maggie seemed to know her way around so well I was beginning to wonder if she was part cat. She darted around the maze of streets, and I made a mental note to stay close to her, because if we got separated right now, I wasn't sure I'd ever find my way back to our place, even with Google Maps handy on my phone.

Before I knew it, Maggie stopped on a dime, and I nearly careened into her. "Here we are," she said, standing in front of a small home.

The front door was dark, but that was about all I could tell. Everything here was dark. "How are we getting in?" I asked.

"You don't know how to pick a lock?" Maggie asked.

I shook my head. "No. Because I'm a normal person."

"I suppose I should admit I can't do it

either," Maggie said. "However, I'd be willing to bet that upstairs window was left unlocked."

I looked up and groaned. "And let me guess: I'm going to be the one responsible for getting up there."

"Youth before beauty," Maggie replied.

I rolled my eyes. "I can't believe you were worried that what I was wearing might attract onlookers compared to scaling the side of a building to try and get through a second-story window."

"Better do it quickly, then," Maggie said.

I looked up the front of the building and realized I had no idea how I was going to do this. I had gone rock climbing exactly zero times. I was low-key scared of heights, and that included climbing the side of a building.

"You better not be suggesting I do this in the hopes that I fall down, split my head open, and you get my half of the inheritance," I warned as I took a careful step forward.

"That's not at all how inheritance law works," Maggie replied.

I grabbed a hold of one of the stones on the exterior of the building. But as hard as I tried, it became quickly obvious that there was no way I was going to be able to scale my way up there. This was not only outside of my comfort zone, this was well past my skill level. This was a traditional Cornish row house; there were windows and doors but no additional architectural features that would allow me to get to the second floor. A gecko might have been able to scale this wall, but I certainly wasn't going to manage it.

"Wait here," Maggie said, disappearing around the side of the house.

I pulled out my phone and did what any good millennial would do: I opened up YouTube and typed into the search bar, "how to pick a front door lock."

I immediately tapped on the top video, which was fourteen minutes long, and scrolled past the first useless seven minutes during which the presenter explained what a lock was, what a door was, and why you might want to break into one. I assumed. Why make a fourteen-minute video when a three-minute one would suffice?

I was just about to announce to Maggie that we had to stop by the store to get a bobby pin when she returned, holding a key triumphantly overhead.

I raised my eyebrows. "Where did you get that?"

"Found it hidden in the garden at the back. What are you doing?"

"Looking up how to pick a lock on YouTube."

"Keep that in mind for the future. It might come in handy. But right now, we're all set." Maggie reached the front door and pulled a pair of latex gloves from her pocket. She handed me a pair, and I slipped them on.

I held my breath as Maggie slipped the key into the lock. She turned it, and the click of the bolt on the inside told me it had worked.

We were in.

As soon as I closed the door behind me, I turned on the flashlight of my phone. "We can't turn any lights on, obviously," I said.

"No. Keep that pointed away from the windows. Let's split up. You take the lower level, and I'll see what's upstairs."

"Take pictures of anything that looks like it might be important."

Maggie nodded. "Will do. Close the curtains when you're in the living room. We don't want anybody calling the police in the middle of the night, alerting them to our presence."

"Got it."

Maggie walked through the front hallway toward the back of the house, and a moment later, I heard the creak of an old staircase. I turned through the first doorway on the right and found myself in what was obviously the living room. I turned off the flashlight as I walked toward the front windows, hitting my knee on the coffee table and letting out a string of expletives on the way.

But a few seconds later, the blinds were closed, and I turned my phone's flashlight back on, scanning around the room to get an overall impression of the place.

This was obviously the abode of a single

man who hadn't been much of an entertainer. Against the wall, behind the coffee table that had gotten in my way was an upholstered love seat that looked as if it had been years since anyone had sat down on it. On the other hand, next to it was a recliner so obviously well used I could have taken an accurate plaster cast of Greg's ass.

Next to it was a side table covered in empty beer bottles on top of an old magazine. On the floor next to it were some empty takeaway containers that were obviously halfway toward creating their own eco-system.

The other side of the room featured a large TV, sitting on a stand with storage beneath it. Leaning against the stand was a cricket bat, and a hoodie was crumpled in the corner next to it. I figured I might as well start with the storage space under the TV. I crouched down onto my haunches as I looked through Greg's things. There were a handful of games for his Nintendo Switch and some DVDs, mainly of eighties action movies. Greg was an Arnie fan, by the looks.

I went through the DVDs, but one of them didn't feel right. I paused, went back to it, and picked up the case. It was heavier than it should have been. I shook it. There was definitely more than just a disk in here.

Opening it up, I found a small notebook. I flipped open the pages and found a list of names and a bunch of numbers next to each of them.

A bookie's record of what people owed him? Maybe. I went to slip it into the pocket of my pants only to realize that I was wearing leggings that only had a tiny pouch large enough for a few credit cards and a driver's license.

Whoops.

I shoved the notebook into the back waistband of my leggings and continued going through all the DVDs, taking extra care now that I knew this was Greg's old hiding spot.

Suddenly, I heard a sound at the front door. I froze, hoping against all hope that my ears had misheard. But no. There was a scraping sound, and it was definitely coming from the entrance. Someone else was trying to break in here.

My eyes widened as panic threatened to grip me. What was I going to do? I immediately got to my feet and grabbed the cricket bat.

"Maggie," I hissed, not daring to speak loudly. "Maggie, someone's trying to break in."

Nothing. There was no reply, and I couldn't call out any louder; if I alerted the intruder to my presence, I would be even more screwed than I already was.

The lock clicked, and I had about two seconds to decide what to do. There was always the possibility that a neighbor had seen us arrive and had called the police.

Somehow, I doubted it. Not only would a cop have entered much more smoothly—this person had obviously picked the lock—but from what I had gathered from Maggie, England wasn't all that different from America. The cops weren't going to prioritize a break-in in the middle of the night, even at the home of a murder victim.

No, this wasn't the police. Not that the cops would have been a *good* option, given that I had definitely broken and entered. This might very well be the killer.

The front door creaked open and I instinctively pressed myself against the wall. I had the cricket bat in one hand, and I quickly brought it up, holding it like a baseball bat as I tried not to breathe. I strained to hear the sound of the intruder, and after a couple of seconds, I heard footsteps coming toward me.

I squeezed my eyes shut, knowing that I was going to have to do this. As the man got closer, I swung the bat, aiming for his chest. I wasn't trying to kill him or anything, just to stun him. I hadn't really thought through what I was going to do next. I hadn't had time to come up with a plan. I was winging it.

I connected with something, but it was like hitting a rock.

"What the——?" a man's voice exclaimed.

I darted out and shoved him as hard as I could against the wall.

Without waiting to see if he was okay, I sprinted toward the front door, but the man reached out and grabbed me by the wrist, stopping me in my tracks. "Who are you?" he asked.

But I yanked myself out of his grasp. I still had the cricket bat in my other hand, and I whipped it around and swung for his leg.

The man let out a cry and let go.

I reached the door, but as I was opening it, I felt resistance. His hand was closing it behind me.

Fear closed my throat as I turned around to face him. "What do you want?" I managed to snarl at him, trying to sound as threatening as possible.

"Who are you? Why are you here?"

As if I was going to answer that.

I was just getting ready to kick out, hoping to make contact with his groin in the dark, when Maggie's voice cut through. "What do you call it when you hit a fool over the head with a frying pan?"

There was silence for a second, and then instinctively, I answered, "What?"

"Dead Benedict. You're going to back up and walk slowly into that living room if you know what's good for you," Maggie said to the man. "And don't make the mistake of thinking I'm not willing to knock your brains out."

"Okay, okay," the man said.

I fumbled around for my phone and turned the flashlight back on to see the man holding his hands up, looking somewhat amused by the whole situation.

He was tall, a couple inches over six feet. He had on a pair of jeans and a black Henley shirt that clung to his body, betraying the fact that he was a regular gym-goer. His wavy, chestnut-brown hair was slightly tousled, and he had a couple days' worth of stubble on his face. His mouth was curved upward in a slightly amused smirk, and his dark eyes glimmered.

He reminded me of a more annoying Pedro Pascal.

I wanted to roll my eyes at him. He was the classic pretty boy who thought he was so much better than everyone else and probably thought he was just placating us. He didn't believe for a second Maggie would have knocked him over the head with her frying pan. She should have done it; then he wouldn't be smirking.

"So," the man said as soon as we entered the living room. He casually strode to the love seat and plonked himself down in the middle of it, stretching his arms across the back. "Who are you two ladies, and why have you broken into a murder victim's home in the middle of the night?"

Chapter 11

"It's adorable how he thinks he's asking the questions here," I said to Maggie. I finally got a look at her. Sure enough, she had a frying pan in one hand and was tapping the bottom gently on the other, like a mafia enforcer who'd use the pan to make a mean carbonara after she was done breaking kneecaps.

"Did you kill Greg?" Maggie asked.

I shined my flashlight directly at him as if I was a police interrogator.

The man turned his head slightly away, squinting, but didn't seem especially bothered by my movement. "It would be pretty stupid of me to come back here if I did, wouldn't it? No, I didn't kill him. But you're the main suspects, aren't you?"

"How do you know that?" I asked.

"When you hear the bookshop is now owned by Carl's mother and his recently-arrived-from-America daughter, given your ages and accents, it's not that hard to put two and two together."

"If you know who we are, then who are you?" I asked. "You're breaking into a murder victim's home in the middle of the night. You know about this case, so you're not just some looter taking advantage. What are you? Someone who owed Greg money?"

The man chuckled, obviously amused. "Name's Aksel."

"What's your last name, Wheel?" I replied.

"Americans. So well known for both your sense of humor and your ignorance. Aksel is a Norwegian name. My mother's homeland. Last name is Evans. I'm a private investigator, hired to find Greg's killer. It appears we have the same goal."

"Hired by who?" Maggie asked.

"Can't say. Privacy reasons." His smirk told me that even if he could, he wasn't going to tell us.

"How do we know you're even telling the truth?" I asked, crossing my arms in front of me. "Frankly, you just broke into a man's home in the middle of the night. I'm not inclined to give you the benefit of the doubt."

"And you attacked me, so why should I answer you?" he replied.

"It was self-defense."

"You broke in here first. You could be up to

no good. And you're the prime suspects, according to the police."

"And if you believed we were the murderers, you wouldn't be here, in Greg's home, looking for evidence," I snapped back.

Aksel laughed. The sound grated against me. He wasn't supposed to be this casual. We were all in a murder victim's home in the middle of the night, and he was acting as if we were having drinks at the bar.

"You're not wrong. Only an idiot would think the two of you had something to do with Greg's death, especially after finding out what the man was into."

"And what might that have been?" Maggie asked.

"Sorry, can't tell you. Secret of the trade."

I pulled out my phone and did a quick Google search. Sure enough, Aksel Evans, Private Investigator, Cornwall. "Okay, let's say we believe you. You're a PI. What do you know? You tell us, and we'll let you out of here."

Aksel leaned forward, resting his elbows on his knees. "Or how about this? I don't tell you anything, and you let me go anyway."

"Nah."

"What do you think you're going to do to me?"

"Have you forgotten about this?" Maggie asked, spinning the frying pan around in one hand.

"Neither one of us really believes you're going to smoke me with that thing."

"Keep talking like that, and you'll find out just how wrong you are," she replied.

"Okay. So the way I see it, we're at an impasse. I'm not going to tell you anything. You're obviously here looking for information as well. Why don't you tell me what you know? I do this professionally. I'm trained to find criminals. You're..."

"Yes?" I replied.

"Well, I don't know what you're trained for."

"I'm a CIA assassin."

"Somehow, I don't believe you."

"Neither did Salvador Allende."

"You were decades away from being born when he was assassinated."

"My makeup is just that good."

"Okay. This is ridiculous. Give me what you've got, and I'll make sure the real killer is found."

Honestly, this guy was so cocky I wasn't going to give him what we had on principle alone. Even if he could help, I'd rather rot in jail than let him find the killer.

"Sorry," I said with a smile. "I don't have any reason to believe you're better at this than we are. I guess we'll see who finds the killer first, won't we?"

"Why don't we leave Aksel here to his investigation? I think I've found everything important upstairs," Maggie suggested.

"Sounds like a plan."

The two of us turned around to leave, and Aksel turned on his own phone flashlight.

"Hey, what's that you've got in your pants? Is it important to the investigation?" he called out after me.

"Stop checking out my ass," I replied without looking back as the two of us left Greg's home.

It wasn't until we were back out in the fresh air and walking home that the gravity of what had just happened hit me.

"He's also looking for Greg's killer," I said quietly.

"It appears that way."

"I looked him up. He is actually a private investigator. That doesn't rule him out as a suspect, obviously, but…"

I trailed off, and Maggie finished the thought for me. "But it makes it less likely, and he really would be a moron for breaking into Greg's home after killing him. So let's say he was telling the truth. Who hired him to find Greg's killer?"

"It could have been Dirk," I suggested. "After all, Greg was important to his business."

"It could have been, but why would he? Greg's death was tragic for him, but he's a businessman. He's not the sort to hire a private investigator unless he thought there was profit in it for him. Not for one of his drivers."

"True," I said, frowning. "Then maybe someone linked to the gambling? There are just too many suspects for now."

When we got home, I settled into one of the old wooden chairs around the small dining table, and Maggie immediately went to the counter to make a pot of tea. I pulled the notepad from the back of my leggings. "This is what Aksel saw as he was checking me out when we left. I found it hidden in a DVD case. I haven't looked at it closely. Did you find anything?"

"Nothing good. I had a look in the two bedrooms upstairs and the kitchen."

"Let me guess, there was virtually nothing in the fridge?"

"Condiments, mostly."

"Going by the state of the living room, Greg was keeping a lot of the takeout places in town in business single-handedly. Sounds about right. Bachelor?"

"I saw no sign of and have never heard of him being in a relationship. So ultimately, I found nothing."

"Well, at least we have this," I said, pulling out the notebook.

I flipped it open to the first page. Sure enough, it was as I'd seen inside the house. On the left-hand side were names, and next to them were numbers. Most of the numbers had been crossed out. Some of the names repeated over and over.

"I don't see Norman on here," I said, my eyes scanning the pages as I flipped through them.

"Let me have a look at that," Maggie said. I handed her the book. "How much did Norman owe Greg again?"

"Ten grand, Dave said."

"This, here." Maggie pointed to a line toward the end of the book. It read, "Hunter – 10k, 15/5"

"I hate to point out the obvious, but Hunter and Norman are two different names. Dave told us Norman's last name was Bally."

"True, but Norman Hunter was a famous footballer back in the day. Part of the team that won the World Cup back in the sixties."

I nodded. "You think that's Greg's code."

"Given as he's named one of them Haaland, I'd say so. It's not exactly a common name around these parts."

"Okay. So we can go through these lists, and at least come up with first names and how much they owed Greg. That's going to give us a nice list of suspects, I would think." I stifled a yawn.

Maggie gave me a sharp look. "You should go to bed. It's been a long day, and I'm sure the jet lag isn't helping. I'll go through this and see what I can come up with."

"That's probably a good idea," I said,

stretching as I stood up from my chair. My eyes were burning, I was so tired.

"I can name more football players than you can, anyway, I'm assuming."

"Hey, if any of them are named Beckham, I can tell you that's a David," I replied with a smile and another yawn. I failed to stifle the second one. "I'll see you in the morning."

"Good night, Mack. And good work tonight getting Aksel when he came through the door."

"I tried to call to you," I said, leaning against the doorframe. "But I didn't want to be too loud in case he heard me coming. I should have hit him harder."

"We live and learn. I am curious who hired him. We'll add that to our list of questions about this case. By the morning, we'll have a plan."

"I hope so," I said, heading up to bed. I hadn't realized how exhausted I was. I had barely collapsed into bed before sleep overtook me.

OF COURSE, THE BEAUTY OF JET LAG IS THAT even when you've been up for way too many hours straight, been interrogated by the police, cleaned blood off the floor, and committed a felony, the brain still goes, "Hey, you should be awake right about now" long before your body agrees.

I woke up the next morning just after seven and made my way downstairs. Maggie was still asleep, like any normal person who went to bed after two would have been, so I grabbed my phone and a handful of cash, threw on a jacket, and went back out to the Ugly Mug Café for a gallon of their strongest coffee.

I walked through the door, and Sophie grinned. "How's it going, babes? Solve your murder yet?"

"Not quite." I sidled up to the front counter and glanced at all the goodies on offer today. My eyes immediately landed on the cookies-and-cream cheesecake. "But if I'm going to jail, a slice of that will help. Also, your strongest coffee. I'll have it here today. I was up late last night."

"Working the case?"

"Yeah. Hey, do you know a guy named Aksel?"

"Aksel Evans? Certainly do. He works as a private investigator now. He came here from London about ten years ago as a young police officer. A few years ago, something went on. I'm not quite sure on the details—it was all kept very hush-hush—but Aksel was forced out. He left the police force, but he stayed in town. Made a new career for himself here. Why? Is he involved in Greg's murder?"

"He's working the case, according to him. Wouldn't tell me who he's working for, though."

"I'll keep an ear out." Sophie grinned.

"You're lucky. Less than two days in town, and you've already met the man all the ladies swoon over."

I rolled my eyes. "Seriously, *that* guy?"

"Hey, what can I say? He's good looking."

"Maybe, until he opens his mouth."

Sophie laughed. "So, I take it the two of you didn't hit it off, then?"

"That's one way of putting it."

"Hey, Ann wanted me to let you know she's going to come by later with some paint. I think she said to be there around ten o'clock."

"Oh, great," I said with a smile. "That's so nice of her to do."

"People around here are really community minded. We help each other out. It's how things have always been done in Cornwall."

"I still need to come up with a name for the place."

"Are you going with a specific theme?"

I pursed my lips. "I'm not sure. I want it to stick out. I want it to be cozy, but I want it to have atmosphere, you know? The kind of place where you feel like you can just curl up with a book and a hot chocolate and sit by the window, watching the rain fall. That's what this place reminds me of."

Sophie nodded. "That's perfect. Yeah."

"It's such a big space, I think it could be used so much better. I want to let more natural light in but keep it from looking bright and fluorescent. I want people to be comfortable, but I want to give the indication that it's not your typical bookstore. I need a name that has a bit of an edge to it."

"Let me think about it. I'll come up with some ideas for a name," Sophie said.

"Sweet, thanks. I'd love to hear them. I'm both excited for what this place can be and trying not to get too attached in case it all, you know, goes away."

Sophie shook her head. "No matter what, it's going to be fine. You're not going to prison for something you didn't do."

"I hope you're right. You said ten o'clock, right?"

"Yes, that's when Ann's going to be back."

"Cool, that leaves me a couple of hours. Listen, do you know where I can find someone named Jeremy Haggerty? Or Norman Bally? Norman has a bit of a gambling problem, and Jeremy probably isn't the most law-abiding citizen you've ever met. He's the one who connected Greg with Dirk, who got him into running drugs."

"Norman owns one of the farms a little ways outside of town," Sophie said. "You'd need a car to get there, no question."

"I haven't quite gotten around to learning to drive on the other side of the road yet. What about Jeremy?"

Sophie shook her head. "Sorry, don't know him."

"It's all good. Maggie's on it, so I'm sure I'll have an answer soon."

"Look, if you want something to do, and you've got a few hours before Ann's going to get back, why don't you go for a short hike? You're new to the area, the weather's gorgeous out today, and it's frankly a shame that you're in one of the most beautiful parts of England and not able to enjoy any of it."

"That's not a bad idea, but honestly, a relaxing walk by the seaside isn't likely going to help when I have a potential murder indictment hanging over me. I was going to go see Johnny at the bank. Open an account and what have you and see what I can find out from him."

Sophie offered me a sympathetic smile. "You're still in big-city mode. The bank doesn't open until ten. And even then, you're lucky. The bank where John works is only open three days a week. And today is one of those days."

"You're joking."

"Nope. You're too much of a city girl."

"I guess a walk in nature is the only thing on the agenda, then," I said with a disbelieving laugh. What kind of bank was only open three days a week and then didn't open until ten? "Got any suggestions for me?"

"Sure," Sophie said. "Here, have a seat. I'll bring you your coffee and cheesecake in just a moment, and we've got some maps around here. I'll show you the best spot."

Maybe Sophie was right. With everything going on, a couple hours in nature couldn't really hurt. Right?

Chapter 12

IMMEDIATELY AFTER I WENT TO SIT DOWN, AN older couple entered the coffee shop, looking slightly dazed, and Sophie set about serving them before getting my drink and cake. Five minutes later, though, she sat down on the chair across from me, sliding over my food and drink and pulling out a map of the area, one of those detachable ones for tourist shops that come in a pack of fifty.

"Okay," she said, pulling out a pen and clicking it open. "We're here. Ugly Mug Café." Sophie drew an X on the map in the center of town then turned the map around so it faced me.

"Now, there's the beach over here, but honestly, who cares? It's May, and I know the water is already turquoise and gorgeous, but trust me, you don't want to be swimming in that water until late in the afternoon, after it's had a whole day to warm up. Unless you're one of those psychopaths who loves swimming in cold water, skip the beach for now."

"Got it. You will not find me in cold water."

"Good. So, instead, I'd say you should head up to Politician's Point. It's about a twenty-minute walk from here. Head over to the beach, and you'll see the trailhead. It's not far from there. That will take you up to the cliffs, and you'll get a gorgeous view over the water. There's also a decommissioned old lighthouse there."

"Why's it called Politician's Point?" I asked.

Sophie grinned. "Rumor is back in the day, they used to throw corrupt politicians off the cliff and into the water. Of course, it's been hundreds of years since that's last happened, at the very least, so who knows how much of it is true and how much of it is local legend?"

"I imagine it serves as a bit of a warning to anyone who's getting too big for their britches, though," I replied.

"It certainly does. Anyway, that's a nice spot to have a look, but if you keep on the path, it'll take you along the cliffs and back down to the water level. There are some beaches, tide pools, that sort of thing. It's quite safe so long as you watch the tides and stay off any wet rocks. You don't want to be swept away."

I grabbed the pen from Sophie and pretended to write on the map. "Don't... die... got it."

Sophie shook her head. "You'd be surprised at how many people ignore the signs warning them of the danger."

"I've worked retail before. I wouldn't be."

Sophie burst out laughing. "You said it, not me. Anyway, when you run out of time, turn around and come back the way you came. But take a jacket. It can be windy on the cliffs and by the water."

"Thanks for this," I said as Sophie stood up again.

"Of course. I'd happily play tour guide if I wasn't in the middle of a shift. But you should enjoy it. I know you've moved here permanently, but it would be a shame for you not to enjoy the natural beauty of Cornwall right off the bat. There's more to this place than murder suspects."

Sophie headed back to the counter to serve more customers, and I pored over the map she'd given me. Sure enough, the route looked pretty interesting. And besides, breathing in some salty ocean air might wake me up a little bit more.

I was going to need all the help I could get in that department today.

I dug into the cheesecake, leaning back and letting out an involuntary moan of pleasure as the soft, creamy interior hit my tongue. Anyone who said sex was better than a good cheesecake was lying, and this was a *very* good cheesecake.

By the time I was finished, I still had a

couple of hours before the bank would open. I texted Maggie, letting her know my plan to see him so she could message me if she had any questions for Johnny. Then I followed the map Sophie had given me and began my walk into nature.

I took a hard left as I exited the coffee shop then turned to walk toward the harbor. I followed the main road for a while then took another left toward the main beach in town. Sure enough, when I reached the parking lot, a sign at the far end indicated the St. Albinus Coast Trail. I passed by the small tourist placard and the box of dog-poo bags for any pet owners who needed them and started on my walk.

Within minutes, my breath was completely taken away by the beauty of this place. As I left the beach, the path sloped upward. Soon, I was standing on a single-track dirt path, surrounded by long green grass being gently guided in every direction by the strong ocean winds.

Dark rocks jutted up here and there, especially toward the edges of the cliffs. Pink, purple, blue, and white wildflowers—none of which I recognized—bloomed along the path, interrupting the greens of the grass with their bursts of color.

To my right, dark cliffs rose up from the turquoise waters of the Celtic Sea that turned a deeper blue the farther I looked from shore. Way out on the water, sunlight glinted off the hulls of fishing boats, like man-made stars.

This was one of the most beautiful places I'd ever seen.

I continued for about ten minutes, letting myself soak in the view as I went, before I reached Politician's Point. The old lighthouse was made of pale, whitewashed stone. It stood about a hundred feet high, with the last twenty feet or so being the glass observation deck, topped with a copper cone roof that had long since patinaed into a color reminiscent of the sea below.

Next to it, the black-and-white flag of Cornwall, St. Piran's cross, blew in the wind, the cloth snapping every few seconds from the force of the bluster.

I joined the handful of other tourists who were up this early at the lookout for a bit then continued on the path.

My phone rang. It was Maggie.

"I thought I'd give you some time this morning to sort yourself out before calling. Where are you?"

"I've gone for a walk. I'm at Politician's Point. Sophie suggested it. I have to be back at the bookstore at ten. Ann is going to bring me some paint. How did your work go, uncovering the gamblers?"

"Decently well. I've got most of them, I think. Hunter, as we know, was Norman. I've cracked the code on a few others also. Haaland isn't referring to Erling, the young Manchester City player. It refers to his father, Alfie. That's bound to be Alfie Kerkin. Fisherman in town; I've known him for decades. Drinks a bit too much but never gets violent. I could see him having a gambling issue. Apparently, he owed Greg two grand."

"Okay. I'd normally say that's not a lot to kill someone over, but you never know."

"Precisely. Then there's DeBruyne. That's got to refer to someone named Kevin, but I don't know anyone by that name in town. Sinclair has to be Jerome Woods. Owner of the grocery store. He was in it for fifteen grand, more than anyone else. And Bergcamp has to be Dennis Grigg, who runs his own general maintenance business out of the back of his van."

My head was spinning. "I hope you wrote all these names down."

"I certainly did. If you're busy with the bookshop, I'll get started with interviews. I'll go and chat with Alfie first; he'll be coming in with the morning catch soon."

"Do you want me to head back and join you?"

"No. I've known Alfie for so long, it will go better if I talk to him alone. Besides, you should enjoy the views of Cornwall. If this is going to be your home, you should explore it."

"Okay, thanks. I'll text you when I'm finished with Ann."

"Are you planning on painting right away?"

"No. I want to help. I was also going to go to the bank and speak to Johnny under the pretense of having to open a new bank account in England."

"Excellent thought. I can meet you there to speak with him as well if I'm done with Alfie."

"Cool."

I said goodbye to Maggie and ended the call, frowning to myself. We had a long list of suspects. I hoped we'd be able to narrow it down sooner rather than later.

It still wasn't even nine o'clock, which meant I had plenty of time to continue before having to be back at the bookshop at ten, so I pressed on.

While there were a few early risers at the lighthouse, and I'd passed a few people here and there along the path, the farther I got from town, the more isolated the trail became. Since I was a city girl, this suited me fine. I was from Seattle, so I was used to getting out into nature, but being so close to a major city meant most of the trails within a day's driving distance generally had a fair bit of foot traffic.

But out here, I was by myself, and it felt good. I listened to the sounds of the wild, especially the birds, whose calls were unfamiliar to me. I'd never imagined myself living in a place where I wouldn't recognize the birds. New York

City, of course, was full of pigeons—or flying rats, as I liked to call them. Seattle had a ton of seagulls—beach chickens—and crows—smart emo birds. But there were also Stellar's Jays—flying punks—finches, and woodpeckers. I

And yet here I was, not recognizing the calls of the birds. I'd have to make up whole new funny names for the ones that lived here. Had I made a horrible mistake? In a way, it felt like yes. Obviously. I was a prime suspect in a murder investigation led by a guy with a potato where his brain should be. But if I got past this, if I could prove my innocence and maybe start a life here, who knew?

I wasn't going to let myself hope for the future until the killer was found, though. I knew better than that.

Sure enough, as Sophie had said in the coffee shop, soon after continuing on past Politician's Point, the trail began to slope down toward the next beach. I had no intention of swimming this early in the day in spring—I was not the kind of person who thought cold plunges did anything to the body other than make you feel like you wanted to die—but I was happy to stand on the sand and watch the water.

I followed the trail down and eventually reached the gorgeous yellow beach. Because it was still early in the morning, and this beach faced west, the tall cliffs on the right-hand side kept the beach clothed in shadow. To the left, the sand eventually turned into rocks. Along the cliff face, I could see numerous small entrances to caverns.

"Yeah, I've seen enough horror movies to know I'm not going there," I said to myself. Instead, I walked along the sand, watching the water. From up above, the gorgeous turquoise mingled with the white crests of waves in a way that made the sea seem welcoming.

Down here, though, it was obvious that the sea was more powerful than it had looked. Waves pummeled the rocks, sending white diamonds soaring into the sky for a split second before falling back down to earth. No wonder Sophie had warned me not to go onto the wet ones. I could see how easy it would be for a single rogue wave to drag someone out to sea, never to be seen again.

When I reached the end of the beach, I spotted a path that rose up some of the higher rocks, out of the reach of the water that led back up toward the main path above the cliffs. They were dry, which meant they were safe, and I crossed over the pools filled with small sea creatures, careful not to step on any of the small crabs running underfoot, and began walking up them.

I obviously wasn't the first person who'd had this idea; there was practically a makeshift path through these rocks made by other hikers.

The ocean just below pummeled the rocks

and cliff face, but I was high enough that at most, all I got was a little mist from the ends of some of the larger waves. It was really cool, though, looking down at the water and seeing what it could do.

The sounds of the waves drowned out the noise from the seabirds, and all I could hear was the water. I stood there for a few minutes, looking out over the sea, before continuing. If I followed the rocks all the way up the cliff face, I could likely rejoin the main trail.

I was about halfway up, still facing the ocean, with the water at least thirty feet beneath me, when I suddenly felt pressure against the back of my shoulders. Someone had just shoved me.

For a split second, I tried to keep my balance, but a second shove between my shoulder blades sealed my fate. I let out a shout as I fell over the edge of the rock and down into the sea below, which was churning like a washing machine in the middle of a spin cycle.

Before I had a chance to even register what was happening, my body plunged into the frigid water.

Chapter 13

I LIKED HOT TUBS. I LIKED SITTING IN THE WARM water, jets all around me, with a glass of white wine in one hand and a bowl of chips within reach of the other.

I was not a fan of cold-water plunges, on the other hand. Nothing against the Finns. I just liked being warm. Especially when that cold water was the Celtic Sea. And *especially* not when she was this angry.

As soon as I hit the water, the frigid liquid made my whole body feel like it was curling in on itself. On the bright side, because my lungs suddenly felt like balloons that had been popped with a knife, my body was incapable of breathing, so I didn't instinctively breathe in any of the seawater.

After a couple of seconds, I forced myself to open my eyes. Above me, I could see light, so I kicked hard, desperate to break through the surface. I did, and I forced myself to inhale a big gulp of air, doing so a split second before a wave broke over me. The force of it sent me back below the surface.

Something hit the side of my body, and I felt skin scraping. Then I realized it wasn't something hitting me. It was me hitting the rocks.

I had to get out of here, or I was dead.

Kicking with everything I had, I breached the surface once more. "Help!" I shouted, water spilling into my mouth, but I knew there wasn't much point. I had been alone on the beach. Or so I'd thought. I didn't have time to deal with the repercussions of what had happened right now, but someone had shoved me off the rocks and into the water.

They had tried to kill me. And right now, there was a good chance they were going to succeed.

No. I refused to let that happen. I refused to let them win. I took a second to get my bearings, spat out the water, then I took a deep breath and plunged below the surface of the water on purpose. The rocks were behind me now, and I pulled my legs toward me like a frog and pushed off them as hard as I could.

Holding my breath, I kicked forward under the water, desperately trying to get away from the rocks. All it would take was for my head to smash against them once, and I was done. It would be over. I needed to get farther away, where I'd have an easier time breathing.

I just had to hope there wasn't some sort of giant whale—or a leather submarine, as I liked to call them—out here in the water, looking for a Mackenzie-shaped snack. I didn't really feel like doing my best impression of my least favorite story in the Bible.

Putting all of my effort in worked, and I soon found myself about thirty feet from the rocks. I turned and began to swim toward the beach, aiming toward the low-lying pools. If I could just get there.

My energy was fading, though, and fast. This wasn't like swimming in the local pool. With every wave, I was fighting the current. It wanted to pull me away from where I was going, and it felt as if I moved one, maybe two feet forward every minute. Plus, my wet clothes were dragging me down.

The shore was so close and yet so far, and I began to understand just how people drowned in the ocean even when they were near the beach.

"Help!" I called out again as my fingers finally scratched at the rocks making up one of the tide pools. But just as I grabbed them, I was pulled away again. "Help!"

There was no point. I kicked as hard as I could, but I was being pulled away. My energy was waning; I no longer had it in me to kick harder. I was going to die here. I wasn't going to make it.

No. Fuck that. I refused to die this way. If I was going to die tragically, it would be doing something stupid of my *own* volition. Whoever had pushed me off that cliff wanted me to give up, wanted me to go under and never come up, and I wasn't going to give them that satisfaction.

I let out a roar, as loud as I could manage, psyching myself up—until halfway through, a rogue wave crashed over me and filled my mouth with water, killing the moment completely.

I spluttered for a moment, spitting the water out and letting the moment make me even angrier. "Go to hell, ocean!" I shouted before feeling one last rush of adrenaline course through me. This was it. This was all I had, but damn it, I was going to save my own life.

I closed my eyes and kicked blindly, as hard as I could, in the direction of the rocks. Again, my fingers scraped against the edge, and I kicked harder, but I was being pulled away again. In between the waves, I kicked once more, and the next thing I knew, I felt something around my wrist.

"I've got you," a woman's voice called out. "Kick! You're almost there."

I used the very last of my energy as I half swam and was half-dragged onto the rocks. As soon as I was on them, I immediately threw up a lungful of saltwater.

"Come on," the woman's voice said. "We have to get out of here. The tide is coming in, and we're at the risk of getting hit by more waves."

My brain was still a muddled mess, but her commanding tone got me to scramble to my feet. The woman immediately wrapped an arm around my waist and helped me as I half ran, half stumbled away from the water toward the caves against the far rocks. I stopped once to vomit up some more seawater. Eventually, the woman stopped near a large boulder and helped me sit down.

"Are you all right? Do you need medical attention? Does anything hurt?"

I blinked hard as I tried to process her words and opened my eyes, looking at the woman who had saved me. Big brown eyes looked at me with concern. Her hair was in a twist out, held back from her face with a thick, white headband. She had on a pair of cute shorts that had a tie in the front and had a T-shirt tucked into it.

"I… I think I'm okay," I answered, although I had no idea if that was true.

"Stay here. I have a towel with my things. Don't move."

I didn't think I could have gotten up even if I'd wanted to. I sat on the rock and focused on my body. Looking down, the first thing I noticed was that every inch of me was soaked. My shirt had a tear down the side, and the skin under it flamed an angry red.

My hair hung down in strands from my scalp. I would have looked not unlike a sea creature from the deep coming out to devour mankind.

But luckily, apart from a massive headache and a burning sensation on my side where the scratches were, I didn't feel any other pain. I had come out of this relatively unscathed.

The woman came running back a moment later, carrying a backpack with her. She looked me up and down when she reached me. "Okay, you're soaked, and it's cool and windy out. You need to get dry right away. Here."

She handed me a large beach towel, which I took gratefully. The woman rifled through her bag as I pulled off my soaking pants and dried my legs, then did the same with my shirt. I was now standing in my underwear in the middle of the beach, which wasn't exactly ideal, but I was dry, which I knew would save me from potential hypothermia.

"Here," the woman said, tossing me a black T-shirt from her bag.

I slipped it on. Luckily, we were pretty similar in size, although she was a bit taller, and the shirt hung low, offering me a bit more privacy.

"I only bring an extra shirt to the beach,

sorry. But you can wrap the towel around you as we walk back. You can't put those pants back on until they're dry. Are you good to walk? If not, we can call Search and Rescue. They can come and get you."

I shook my head. "No, I think I'm good. Thanks. Cuts and bruises mostly. Thank you. Shit. You saved my life."

"I did what anyone would have done. I was worried you were already dead when I saw you."

"Where were you? On the beach?"

The woman shook her head. "No, in the caves back there. I was gathering some specimens, but it doesn't matter. Here, have some water."

She passed me a bottle, and I realized as she spoke that while she sounded British, there was a slight American lilt to her accent. I drank greedily, my body grateful for hydration that wasn't mixed with salt.

"Thanks. I think I'm okay to walk, but can we just rest here for a second?"

"Of course. Whatever you need. Can I call someone for you?"

"Oh, shit. Maggie. Umm, I don't know her number off the top of my head."

I rifled around the soaking wet pants and reached into my pocket. By some miracle, my phone was still in it. The screen had been smashed to pieces, spiderwebs of broken glass shooting out from the point of impact in the bottom left corner, but when I tapped it, it flashed to life.

"I guess Apple really means it when they say these things are waterproof for an hour," I said, barking out a laugh.

"Can I ask what happened?"

"Yeah. Someone tried to kill me."

The woman gasped. "You're joking."

"Nope. I was walking up the rocks over there, back toward the path, when I felt someone push against my shoulders. They shoved me twice, into the water. There's no way it was an accident."

The woman's eyes widened as her face paled. "I can't believe it. Who would do something like that?"

"The same person who killed Gregory Hamlisch is my bet," I said dryly. "Give me a second. I need to call my grandmother and let her know whoever did this might be coming after her too."

"What? Of course. Yeah."

"What's your name?" I asked the woman. "I'm Mack."

"Ada," she replied as the phone dialed.

I pressed the speaker button a second before Maggie's voice called out through the speaker. "Hello?"

The sound was faint and sounded slightly garbled. I was definitely going to need a new phone.

"Maggie? It's me. Someone just tried to kill me. I'm okay, and I'm coming back into town, but be careful."

"I'm always careful," she replied. "Are you still in danger now?"

"No. I don't think so. I'm with someone, she's helping me. I'm going to come back home before I go to the bookstore."

"I'll see you there. Be careful, Mack."

"I will."

I ended the call and stood up. Wrapping the towel around me like a skirt, I finally took it all in. "So what brings you out here on a day like this?"

Ada laughed. "Oh, no way. You can't tell me someone tried to kill you, call someone named Maggie to warn her she might also be in danger, and not tell me what this is all about."

"Fair enough. Here's the CliffsNotes version." By the time I was finished, Ada and I were on the path heading back toward town, the way I'd come down. Every few seconds I checked behind me, just in case.

"So you think the murderer followed you this morning?" Ada asked.

"I do. I must not have noticed, but then, I wasn't exactly expecting someone to follow me and kill me. I thought I was alone this whole time. How did you find me?"

"I heard a call from the water. It sounded almost like a whale in distress. I ran out to see what was going on, and that's when I saw you floating on the water. I thought you were dead until I saw your feet kicking, and then I just acted on instinct."

"A whale in distress? Really?"

Ada shrugged, looking a little bit bashful. "You asked."

"You could have lied and said you thought you heard a beautiful mermaid singing. But your instincts saved my life," I said with a smile. "Thank you again."

"Don't mention it. I'm just glad I wasn't too late. So, do you know who this killer was?"

We passed a couple wearing athletic shorts and carrying hiking poles, with matching Camel-Baks on. They looked at my current attire disapprovingly, so I flipped them off as I walked past.

I was sure they wouldn't be looking so athletic if someone had shoved *them* into the water this morning.

"I'm not sure yet. I suppose it can't have been Alfie if Maggie was talking to him. So I'll confirm with her, but we might have one suspect crossed off the list. Other than that, it's still pretty open. I guess we can look for alibis, though. Was anyone out here, trying to kill me, around nine fifteen this morning?"

Ada nodded. "That should hopefully help you narrow it down, especially since you don't have an exact time of death for Greg."

"Exactly. And innocent people are more

likely to have an alibi in the middle of a weekday than sometime during a random night. Most people are sleeping then. So hopefully this will help. But now, I have to find them before they come back to finish the job."

"They obviously wanted to make it look like an accident," Ada mused. "I don't think they'll try anything openly."

I nodded. "I agree."

"You know what else gets me about your case?"

"No, what's that?"

"Why was Gregory Hamlisch killed in the bookstore? Why was he there? Why was *that* where he was murdered. Like, presumably he had to meet his murderer there. But why? Was there a connection between the murderer and Carl?"

I nodded slowly. "That's a really good question."

"I think if you can figure that out, you might be able to narrow things down further."

"You're right. That's good thinking."

"I spent half my childhood reading Agatha Christie, Nancy Drew, anything vaguely mystery-like I could get my hands on," Ada said with a smile.

Just then, I froze. Coming toward us was another person, but this wasn't an ordinary tourist going for a morning hike.

It was Aksel.

Chapter 14

"Who?" Ada asked quietly.

"Private investigator, supposedly, looking into this case too."

"And he just happens to be here, on the same path as you, less than fifteen minutes after someone pushed you into the ocean?" Ada's voice sounded skeptical.

"My thoughts exactly," I muttered as we approached the man. Seeing him in full daylight was different from last night, when he had been illuminated only by my phone's flashlight.

Today, he wore a fitted polo shirt and a pair of slacks. His wavy hair still had that tousled look, and his cheekbones were even more prominent during the day. There was no doubt he was hot. Annoyingly so. And he might have tried to kill me.

"You," I said as he approached. I watched his reaction carefully.

A flash of surprise crossed his face, but it was quickly replaced by a confident grin.

"Mackenzie, is it? You'll forgive me. I asked around and found out your name this morning." He then looked me up and down. "A bit early in the season to go for a swim, I would think, but then I don't know how you do things in America."

"Oh, that's cute. First, you try to drown me, and now, you're making little quips."

A cloud of confusion passed over Aksel's face. "Tried to drown you?"

"Don't play dumb with me. Do you really think I believe that someone pushed me into the ocean and you just *happen* to be walking in the same area right after? That this is all just some sort of coincidence?"

"When did this happen?" Aksel's voice asked, his voice carrying a sharp undertone. "And where, exactly?"

"She doesn't owe you answers," Ada chimed in, reaching over and taking my hand protectively.

"Damn right I don't. What are you doing here, if you claim it wasn't to try and end me? And why did you want me out of the way? Is it because you really killed Greg?"

Aksel shook his head. "Don't be ridiculous. I'm out here because one of the reasons I stayed in Cornwall is because of the natural beauty in this area. I thought I'd go for a walk and think about this case. I certainly wasn't here to do anything to you. I had no idea you were even out here."

"You'll forgive me if I don't believe you," I said dryly.

Aksel looked me up and down as if realizing for the first time the gravity of the situation. "If you've been in the water, you're going to catch cold. We need to get you warmed up. My van isn't far. We can take it, and you can get warm. I'll take you back home."

An incredulous laugh escaped me while Ada shot him a disbelieving look. "You *must* be joking. Believe it or not, we aren't damsels in distress. We've got everything covered, and the last person Mack is accepting a ride from is a man she believes to be a suspect in her own attempted murder. Now, if you don't mind, you're right that every minute is of the essence, and I'll be getting her safely where she needs to be."

Ada stepped forward, and Aksel took a step off the path to let us pass. Still, he was so close when I walked past that I could feel the heat emanating off him. I couldn't help but wonder: was I looking my attempted killer in the eye?

"Mackenzie?" Aksel called when we were about twenty feet away.

I turned to look at him. "Yes?"

"Be careful. And I preferred your ass in those leggings." He shot me a grin.

I narrowed my eyes at him and flipped him

off before turning and sauntering further down the trail.

"Men," Ada said derisively, shaking her head. "You didn't mention him before. Was he one of your suspects?"

"Sort of. Not really. But he sure as hell is now. I knew he was a private investigator, and I knew he was looking into this case, but I thought that was it. We ran into him, uh, the other day while looking for some evidence. I believed his story that he'd been hired to look into this case, and that was why he came across it. But now?"

"The timing is certainly suspicious," Ada said. "But why would he be coming toward us instead of leaving? You'd think if he had pushed you, he'd be getting out of here as fast as he could."

"He's arrogant enough to believe that he succeeded and that he wouldn't get caught."

"Okay, I can believe that," Ada agreed. "He's on the suspect list for sure."

"I don't like him. There's something off about him. Sophie said he used to be a cop here in town but that something happened a few years ago, and he quit the force. Still lives here, though."

"I wouldn't know anything about that. I'm new to town; only lived here for about eighteen months."

"What brought you here?"

"Work. I'm a chemical biologist. I study the

biology of marine life and the chemical structure of its nature to determine ways to improve the lives of people."

My eyebrows flew up. "Okay, so you're *smart* smart."

Ada chuckled. "I know my field, at any rate. I work at the university here, where I do my research."

"You said you were out here collecting specimens. You weren't just being a weirdo, you're an actual scientist."

"I am. Although weirdos can contribute to science as well."

"Fair enough. You work for the university?"

"Yes. Lisle University is one of the most important research universities in England, and they're one of the top spots for the specific kind of research I do."

"That's really neat. Do I hear a bit of an American accent, though?"

Ada smiled. "Well spotted. I did my last few years of high school and all of my undergraduate studies in America. I went to Columbia, and after seven years in the States, a bit of the accent stuck."

"My last job was in New York City," I replied. "Before moving here. I was fired so that the CFO's daughter could take my job, a couple of weeks after my team won a national advertising award for a campaign I spearheaded. And thanks to at-will employment laws, there was nothing I could do. I was annoyed at the time, obviously, but it gave me the perfect reason to come out here. I'm still not sure if it was the right call. I guess I'll have to see if I'm still alive and free in a week."

"I'm sure you will be."

Ada showed me a shortcut to get back to the edge of town, and before I knew it, we were back on the street. I thanked her again and said goodbye, we exchanged phone numbers, and I promised to keep her up to date on the case.

Soon, I was back home. My feet were blistered from having walked in the wet shoes the whole way. It hadn't been so bad when I was walking along with Ada and on the dirt path, which had cushioned them somewhat. But now that I was alone and on the concrete, I was all too aware of the squelching sound that acted as sound effects for every step I took.

As soon as I entered the house, Maggie rushed out to greet me. She looked me up and down. "Straight to the shower with you."

I nodded, relief flooding over me because I was finally home. I turned the water as hot as it would go and stepped into the tub then realized that was a terrible idea and made it just a little bit cooler. I let the water flow over me, warming me to my bones. After about ten minutes, I stepped out, got dressed, and went back downstairs. I had to be at the bookstore in less than a quarter of an hour.

"Someone's trying to kill us," I announced. "Well, me, at least. And I think it might be that private investigator we met last night."

"Oh? He's not searching for the killer because he *is* the killer?"

"I ran into him on the path, just a few minutes after I was shoved into the water. It might have been a coincidence, but I don't like coincidences."

"Coincidence is Fate's favorite tool," Maggie agreed.

"Sure. So anyway, I think we need to look into him more closely. What did you say you knew about him? He used to be a cop here?"

"Yes. He transferred from London when he was a young man, and he worked in this area. A few years ago, there was some sort of scandal within the police force. I'm afraid I don't know the details. They kept it very hush-hush, but Aksel quit."

I scowled. "Maybe they found out he was willing to take the law into his own hands."

"It's possible. I'll see what I can uncover. I have a few people I can ask who might know some details."

"Great. Because right now, whoever killed Greg has their sights on me, which means you're probably also in their crosshairs. We have to get to the bottom of this, and fast. I'm going to go meet Ann at the bookstore, then I'll go to the bank and speak with John. You spoke with Alfie this morning?"

Maggie nodded. "He couldn't be the killer; I left him about a minute before you called. I was speaking to him when the killer was coming after you. Besides, I don't believe it was him. Alfie's got terrible arthritis now. I saw him down at the dock, trying to handle the boxes, ropes, and tools. He can barely do it. I don't think he'd have been capable of grabbing a knife and plunging it into Greg."

"Good. That's at least one suspect crossed off our list."

"And I spoke to Jeremy Haggerty as well. It couldn't have been him. He's on holiday in Thailand with his wife. Sent me a picture with yesterday's paper in case I didn't believe him. He's not in the country. I'll come with you to see Ann and go to the bank."

We left and walked the few blocks to the bookstore. Ada's question followed me as soon as I laid eyes on it. Why had that been the location chosen to murder Greg? Why had two people met in an abandoned bookstore in the middle of the night?

A second later, I spotted Ann, who motioned me over. "My car's parked a few streets away," she explained. "Good, Maggie's here too. Come and have a look. I grabbed all the paint I could find from my brother's place, and he said you're more than welcome to it. If you don't like the color, no harm no foul, but if you do, it could save you a fair bit of cash."

"Thanks again," I said gratefully.

We followed Ann through a nearby alley about a block over—I had to guesstimate because the squiggly, curvy roads here in Cornwall were nothing like the square blocks I was used to. Because the bookstore was in the pedestrian-only part of town, she couldn't park directly in front of the store. Ann led us to a five-year-old Toyota parked in a loading zone. Black, the car was in good condition apart from a small hole near the back left tire that had rusted over slightly. She pulled out the keys and pressed the button, and the car beeped as the trunk popped open.

On top of a blue tarp to protect from spills, were four gallon-sized cans of paint. Dried drips on the lids and down the sides showed the exact shade of the paint. It was very pale, nearly white, but with a slight beige tint, adding a hint of warmth to the tone.

"That's perfect," I gushed. "This is exactly what I want for the walls."

"Great. They're yours. I haven't got any rollers or anything though. Sorry."

"This is already a massive help. Thank you."

With Ann and Maggie's help, the three of us got the paint cans into the bookstore. We sat them down on the floor on top of the tarp.

Ann promised to send her husband around

that afternoon sometime to give me a hand with anything I needed that required a bit of muscle and knowledge of how power tools worked. The next thing I knew, she'd left, and Maggie and I were walking through the front doors of the bank.

My grandmother marched right up to the teller and announced, "My granddaughter is here from America, and she needs to open a bank account. We'd like to speak with John Williams."

The teller gave her a tight smile. "I'm afraid the manager's role doesn't involve opening new accounts."

"Don't you give me any guff, Tonya. I know your mother, and I can call her right now and tell her how you're treating me. Given the legal implications with cross-border taxation and the multiple accounts Mackenzie will need to set up —both business and personal—I think John can make the time to meet with her, don't you?"

Maggie's tone indicated that she wasn't going to take no for an answer, and the teller paused for a moment before replying, "Why don't you take a seat at those chairs over there, and I'll see what I can do."

"Thank you very much," Maggie said with a beaming smile. She led me to the seats in question. So far so good.

About five minutes later, a man approached us. Standing just a shade under six feet tall, he wore a smart suit and carried himself with the swagger of a man in his early twenties who thought he was hot shit. He was obviously trying to grow a beard, but it was weak and uneven, reminding me of patches of grass trying to force their way through cracks in the sidewalk. His mouth was serious, his lips pressed together, and his blue eyes looked at us with a look of superiority, as if we weren't good enough to deserve his attention.

"Johnny Williams?" Maggie asked.

"It's John. I've been told the two of you requested a meeting with me," the man said as we stood up. "You're here to open a bank account?"

"Multiple accounts, yes," Maggie replied coolly.

"We have two associates on hand today who can help you with that."

"I'm sure they can. But what they can't do is tell us about Gregory Hamlisch, how he conned you into committing fraud in his name, and where you were the night he was killed to convince us you're not the murderer."

John froze, blinking at us multiple times. It was as if he was a frozen computer.

"What is that, Morse code?" I asked. "Just answer the questions."

"I have nothing to say to you. You're not with the police. You're simply meddlesome locals sticking their noses where they don't belong."

"Greg was killed on our property," I said. "We have a vested interest in finding his killer. Now, you can either talk to us, or we can go right to the police and tell them everything we've learned about you and how Greg managed to convince you to break the rules. You're already in trouble with your bosses up in London, or so we've heard. Do you really want word getting back to them that the police were in here, talking to you about a murder case too?"

John jutted out his chin and shifted his jaw from side to side. "No. You know what? No, I'm not talking to you. I don't have to. If you want to open a bank account here, fine. But I'm not getting roped up in this. They told me Cornwall would be easy. It's just retirees from London and farmers. But you're all nuts. I don't trust you. I don't trust any of you."

"And you shouldn't," Maggie said. "We're not trustworthy."

"Especially not Maggie," I said.

"She's right. In fact, I think I'm going to pop right down to the police station when we leave here and tell them I saw John in front of the bookshop that night."

John opened and closed his mouth a few times, his face reddening in anger. "I wasn't!"

"As far as the police will know, they'll have a lead to follow up on. And who do you think they're going to believe? The retired old woman who's lived here her whole life and grew up with half the town or the newcomer from London in his fancy suit who's probably got his diploma on his office wall and doesn't know anyone in town? In case you're too thick to figure it out, I'll tell you: they're going to believe me. So I suggest you speak with us."

"This is blackmail," John snarled.

"Yes, that is correct," I said. "And it's working."

"This isn't right."

"There are a lot of things in this world that aren't right," Maggie said. "But we do them anyway. Now, you're acting like we're enemies, but you need to shift your mindset here. We can help you. If you didn't kill Greg, tell us everything you know, and we can rule you out as a suspect."

John snorted. "What, *you* think you're going to find the real killer?"

"I'd love to hear why you think we can't," I said, my voice coated in false sweetness.

"Just… you know what, never mind."

"Good answer," Maggie chimed in.

"My office is this way. I can give you five minutes."

We stood up, and I raised my eyebrows at Maggie behind John's back as we followed him deeper into the building. The bank here was small, and so was John's office. It was a standard bank manager's office. Desk, chair, computer, filing cabinet, white walls. A diploma from

University of Greenwich. I bit back a smile when I saw it.

Maggie and I sat down in the two visitor's chairs, which I couldn't help but notice were set a couple of inches lower than John's, so he sat a bit higher than everyone else.

John looked like he wanted to start talking, take over the conversation, and start it on his terms, so I interrupted before he had a chance.

"Now, why don't you tell us how Gregory Hamlisch screwed you over and convince us that you're not the one who shoved a knife into his chest?"

Chapter 15

AT THOSE WORDS, JOHN'S FINGERS, WHICH HAD been casually curled around the edge of the desk, pressed in on it, the tips turning white. He was trying to hide it, but my words had hit a nerve.

"How do you know about that?" he snapped in response.

"This is a small town, John. I'm sure things are different in London, where everyone minds their own business, but people talk here. We know what's going on with everyone. And we know that you got in trouble with your higher-ups in the City when you allowed something to happen you shouldn't have, but you were swindled by Greg. You're not the first person to have that happen to them. I'd say you wouldn't be the last, but, well, it's possible you might have been. And that gives you quite a strong motive to kill him."

John's weight shifted in his chair, causing the plastic to creak slightly beneath him.

"We understand that he was a swindler," I explained, trying to make John feel better. After all, he was still a young guy, fresh out of college, who thought he knew everything. It wouldn't be easy for him to admit he got duped. "It's not your fault. He's been doing this to people for decades. But we need to know what happened."

John shifted his jaw from side to side again. "Fine. You know what? Everyone else seems to already bloody know about this, so why not you too? They're probably going to take this job away from me regardless, so I might as well, at the very least, keep my own arse out of jail in the meantime. You want to know what Greg did? He comes in here, and he has a whole bunch of documents from a company he owns. They all look completely legitimate. He opens his accounts, and then he tells me he wants to apply for a line of credit. I tell him sure, we can do that. But we need income statements."

"And let me guess, they were faker than last week's WWE wrestling match?" I said dryly.

"I didn't know that at the time. They looked real. He had HMRC documents and everything."

"Our equivalent of your IRS," Maggie explained to me.

"There were no red flags. Believe me, I was trained extensively to look for them. But everything with Greg seemed on the up-and-up. One of the tellers came by later and told me that I should double-check everything Greg gave me, but I saw no reason to."

"Right. You thought she had no idea," I said.

John rubbed the back of his neck. "I'm embarrassed about that. I did think to myself she wouldn't know a thing, she was just a teller. I put the documents through, the loan came through, Greg maxed out the line, and the next thing I know, he's not making payments on it. He defaulted, we go to collect, but there's nothing to collect. It was all fake."

"What did he use as collateral?" Maggie asked.

"A warehouse supposedly full of copper in Poland," John said, wincing. "We're not really supposed to do that, but…"

"Greg charmed you into it," Maggie finished.

"Exactly. He seemed so genuine. I thought there was nothing to worry about. But look, I didn't kill him. He got a little over a hundred grand out of the bank, and I got in trouble. I almost lost my job over it. That's true. I don't deny that. I was humiliated in front of my bosses, but they ultimately understood it was a rookie mistake. I'm still here. I moved on. I didn't kill him."

"Where were you the night Greg was killed?" I asked.

"At home. Sleeping. By myself. Didn't know I'd need an alibi."

"And this morning?" Maggie asked. "Before you came to work."

"Why do you need to know about that?" John asked, his brow furrowing.

"That's our business," I replied. "But answering might go a long way in clearing your name."

John's eyes narrowed slightly. I could tell he was still less than thrilled about having to talk to us. He wanted to kick us out of his office, tell us to disappear, and never see us again.

Too bad for him that wasn't an option.

"I was home," John said. "Alone. I wasn't aware I was going to need an alibi. I came to work at nine thirty, as scheduled."

Nine thirty made the timeline tight but not impossible. He could have shoved me into the ocean and gotten back here in time. My eyes moved down to John's shoes. They were pristine. If he'd been wearing them on the dirt path, it would show. But he could have changed shoes here too.

"All right," Maggie said. "Well, thank you for your time. Now, if you don't mind, Mack really does need to get her new bank accounts opened."

John sniffed hard, his air of superiority back. "As you've been told, I'm far too busy to handle opening bank accounts. I'll have one of the other customer service agents help you. Now, you won't be going to the police and telling them I did this, will you? I'd really rather not find myself in more trouble with my employer than I already am."

"Just one more thing. How much was the loan for, exactly?" I asked.

"One hundred and twenty thousand pounds."

"All right, thanks."

Maggie and I left the office and went back to the chairs in the waiting area.

"What do you think?" Maggie whispered to me as we waited.

I shrugged. "Nothing to say he did it for sure. But nothing to say he didn't, either. His ego obviously took a bruising, but is that enough to kill someone? I'm not sure. I didn't get a violent killer vibe from him, but who knows?"

"I agree. I wish he had an alibi. That would have made things so much easier."

Before I had a chance to respond, a woman strode toward us, a massive smile on her face. She introduced herself as one of the customer service agents who would be helping me open my bank account.

An hour later, armed with a glossy folder printed with the bank's logo and filled with the official documentation marking my new bank account, Maggie and I headed home.

"Do you want to go out to the farm and

speak to Norman before you get back to the shop?" Maggie asked.

I nodded. "Yeah. That sounds good. I don't have a timeline on the bookstore, and besides, if we don't find the killer, it's not like I'm going to be able to open anyway. How are we going to get to the farm?"

"I have a car. We'll take it."

"You still drive?"

"Of course I do. Why wouldn't I?" Maggie narrowed her eyes at me as if daring me to suggest she was too old to still be on the roads.

"No reason," I replied quickly.

"WHERE DID YOU GET YOUR DRIVER'S LICENSE, a box of Wheaties?" I shouted. I reached forward to grab the dashboard in a futile but desperate attempt to stop myself from careening into the side door as Maggie yanked the steering wheel to the right. She took a sharp turn around fifty miles an hour faster than the laws of physics deemed possible.

I gritted my teeth as my head bounced off the window of the faded yellow Volvo, which was older than I was but whose interior parts obviously rivalled those of an F1 racecar. The narrow roads of St. Albinus seemed even smaller than usual as Maggie sped along them, stone walls marking property lines only inches away from the side of the car.

"Oh, relax," Maggie replied, taking a hand off the steering wheel.

A small gurgle escaped my throat as I saw that she now only had one hand on the wheel.

"I've been driving along these roads my whole life."

"Minus the parts where your license got taken away, I assume?" I replied, trying to decide what was scarier: seeing everything coming at me at hyperdrive, as if I was in the *Millennium Falcon*, or shutting my eyes and not seeing my oncoming death.

"That only happened twice. And once wasn't even my fault."

"Oh, I'd *love* to hear why you think that. Car! Car, there's a car coming the other way!"

"I see it, I see it," Maggie replied calmly. She yanked the steering wheel to the left to avoid the Land Rover coming the other way. Two wheels rose up onto the sidewalk with a jolt, and we sped past the car, which honked at us on the way.

"Go back to London if you can't handle a real driver," Maggie shouted at him, rolling down the manual window and throwing her arm out to flip him off.

"Can't I go more than one day in this country without almost dying?" I whimpered in my seat. "Just one day. That's all I ask."

"Relax. They obviously never taught you how to drive in America."

"I have ridden in New York City taxis that have scared me less than this."

Maggie reached a roundabout and nearly put the car on two wheels to get around it before speeding through the third exit. We careened up a hill and turned right onto a one-way road.

There was just one problem. The cars parked along the side were all facing the other way.

"You're going the wrong way up a one-way street," I half shouted, half sobbed. "Oh my God, we're going to die."

"It's a shortcut."

"Yeah, a shortcut to the pearly gates."

"Stop being so dramatic. If you drive faster through it, you're less likely to meet a car going the other way. Besides, it's eleven o'clock, and I happen to know no one uses this stretch of road then."

"Oh, sure, yeah, that's definitely how roads work. Everyone is always on them at a precise time every day."

"If you were just going to spend this whole trip whining, I could have left you home."

"If I knew you were going to be trying out for the next *Fast and Furious* movie, I would have accepted."

"I wish. Vin Diesel, now I wouldn't mind seeing how he handles a gear stick up close."

"Ew, Maggie. Ew."

Maggie turned to look at me, narrowing her eyes. "Are you just saying that because I'm old?"

"No, I'm saying it because you're my grand-mother. And please, for everyone's sake, eyes on the road. We can't prove Norman killed Greg if we're dead first."

"I've been driving my whole life, and I'm still here."

"Really? Because it feels like someone just gave you a copy of *Grand Theft Auto* fifteen years ago, and you decided that's how a person was supposed to drive," I replied.

Then I let out a squeal that matched the tires as we exited the one-way road and emerged onto a single-lane road that looked like it hadn't gotten an upgrade since the late nineties. But as soon as the road opened up, the view was phenomenal. The glimpses of it I got as Maggie drove, anyway.

The town of St. Albinus was behind us, and in front were low, rolling hills as far as the eye could see. Green fields on either side were bordered with fences and shrubs, and horses in the paddock next to us watched lazily as we flew past.

Above us, the azure sky was dotted with white whisps of clouds while the sun beat down, bright without being overly hot. It was a perfect late-spring day. Apart from riding in a vehicle with a grandmother who had a death wish.

"This isn't NASA. We don't have to get airborne. It's okay if we stay in this layer of the atmosphere," I said, but Maggie wasn't listening. These roads were so narrow, every time we reached a corner, I saw that a mirror had been installed so drivers could see if there was anyone coming around the other way.

Before long, even the mirrors disappeared. Luckily, we didn't see another car oncoming until eventually, Maggie slammed on the brakes. She jerked the steering wheel to the left and turned onto a dirt driveway that had obviously just been part of a field that had been driven over so many times there were a couple of ruts in the ground.

Small pieces of gravel crunched beneath the tires as we drove toward the large corrugated-iron shed in the distance. As we got closer, I saw this was home to a veritable graveyard of farm machinery. Rusted-out skeletons of what had once been tractors dotted the land around the shed, interspersed with piles of old tires in every size known to man.

Maggie slowed the car to a stop in front of the shed, whose large bay doors were wide open. A man stepped out a moment later, wiping his hands on a rag and squinting to see who had arrived.

"Is that Maggie Summers? Wasson shag? How are you holding up?"

"Hello, Norman," Maggie replied. "This is Mack, my granddaughter."

I got a good look at the man as his gaze shifted to me. He was in his sixties, probably, although the sun damage to his skin could have made him look older than he really was. His bird's nest of hair was grey with specks of brown, and his broad shoulders betrayed that even under the extra fifty pounds he carried, this was a man who worked outdoors all day and had a solid mass of muscle to show for it.

He wore a ragged old pair of jeans, a black T-shirt whose collar had worn out probably ten years ago, and boots so muddy there was no way I'd ever be able to discern the original color. But his face lit up as soon as he saw Maggie, and he grinned a half-toothed smile as he walked toward us.

"Mack, is it? That must make you Carl's daughter. He never said a word to any of us."

"Nor me," Maggie replied. "All the same, she's the one who found Greg's body in the bookshop the other day."

"Oh, wouldn't know nothing about that," Norman replied.

"It's more believable if you wait until we ask you about that to deny it," Maggie replied dryly.

"The way people are these days, they'll accuse you of anything. You can't think I had anything to do with Greg's death. Barely knew the man. You know me, Mags. I wouldn't do a thing like that."

"Maybe not, but you can help us find who did," she said.

Norman looked over at me again. "You got his nose, you know?" he said to me. "Carl's. And his chin. Rest of you, though? Must be the mum."

"I've got her eyes and mouth. And her hair," I replied.

"Good. No way a young woman like you would be happy having Carl's hair. Or should I say, lack of it," Norman said with a grin.

I laughed. I liked the man immediately, but I also kept in mind that I could have been looking at the man who had tried to kill me this morning.

"So, what do you need to know about Greg?"

"Why'd you owe him ten grand, and did you kill him to avoid paying it?"

Norman paused where he was then let out a low whistle. "Cutting right to the chase, are you? How'd you find out I was in deep with Greg? Ah, it was Dave. Of course it was. That man pretends to stand behind the bar, minding his business, but he's got more gossip to trade in than *The* bloody *Sun*."

"It doesn't matter where we got the info. And don't worry, it's safe with us," I said. "But we need to know the details. Why did you owe Greg so much money? Was it from gambling?"

Norman eyed us both. "You're really trying to find the person who killed Greg, aren't you? Wouldn't have believed it, but here we are."

"We have a vested interest in the truth coming out, and do you really think Peters is going to be the one to solve it?" Maggie replied.

Norman grunted. "Fair point. Who am I to stand in your way? Certainly wasn't me who killed him. I owed him, yes. But I was getting the money. I'm up to seven grand I was ready to give him, and I knew Greg. He'd loan me out the rest."

"Can you prove that?" Maggie asked.

"Sure, sure. Let me just get me phone out. Look, I don't know how these app things work, but the one for my bank, it's on here. Just give me a moment."

Norman pulled out his phone and began tapping the screen, although "mashing" was probably a better descriptor. He reminded me of my mother the first time she got a phone, hitting the buttons as hard as possible and leaving her fingers on them for two to three seconds. It made me want to snatch the phone out of his hand and do it for him, as I was sure younger people in his life had done multiple times.

After a minute, though, Norman showed the phone to Maggie. "There. My bank account balance. Just over seven grand. I sold a few things I had lying around. Why would I have bothered if I was just going to kill the guy? No, I didn't do this."

"Okay," Maggie said. "Looks good. But why don't you help us find out who did? Give us some information. You were betting with Greg? What sport? How long had he been doing it? What's the setup? Why go to Greg instead of just betting online?"

"Been betting with Greg for about six months now. As to why, well, that's an easy one. Greg was willing to front me the money. Look, I know, it's not the smartest thing in the world, going into debt for gambling. But I thought I had a sure thing going. I had a plan: I was going to bet on Manchester City winning every game this season. I mean, come on. They've won the title two years running, and they've got Haaland, which should practically be considered cheating. I thought it was a sure thing. They'd win nearly all their games, and even if I was making only a few quid a game, it would add up."

"But going by the fact that you owed Greg cash by the time he died, I'm guessing it didn't pan out that way?" I asked.

Norman rubbed the back of his neck sheepishly. "It started off well. And then I may have got a bit too confident and strayed away from my plan a bit. Made a few bets that weren't quite as good, got myself into a bit of a hole, thought I'd dig my way out of it, but you know how it is."

"It's easy to get in over your head," Maggie agreed.

"That's right. But as I say, I was nearly there. I'd have paid him off, and I'd learned my lesson. No more gambling for me. Not when I didn't have the cash in hand, anyway. But now, as to how it all worked, I'm afraid, Maggie, I've got some bad news for you on that front."

"Me?" My grandmother's eyebrows rose, looking surprised. "Why's that?"

"Greg wasn't working alone in the gambling business, you see. He had a partner. And that man was Carl."

Well, that was certainly unexpected.

Chapter 16

"Carl Summers?" I asked. "As in, my father, ran-the-local-bookstore Carl?"

Norman nodded. "Yes indeed. He was running this gambling outfit with Greg. Though he was more on the back end of things. I gather he was running the money through the book-shop to clean it and make it look slightly more legitimate."

Maggie shook her head. "If he wasn't dead, I'd be having a word with him. I'm half tempted to dig him up and ask him all the same what on earth he was thinking."

"He wanted a quick and easy payday is my thought," Norman replied. "I gather the book-shop wasn't doing the amount of business he wanted, and he was looking for an additional income stream. Greg had his latest idea, and the two decided they could scratch each other's backs."

"I'm curious. You obviously knew about Greg's reputation as a bit of a weasel. Why did you still go ahead and gamble with him? Was it really just about him fronting you the money?"

Norman shrugged. "Ah, it's the vice, isn't it? I thought I had a way to make money, and I thought why not? A couple of years ago, the government banned the use of credit cards on gambling sites, so there's no way to go through the proper channels if you want to have a punt without putting up the cash. Greg wasn't offering odds that were quite on par with most of the online sites, but he wasn't far off, either."

So that was how Greg had been luring people into his scheme. He was promising to front them the money they used to gamble with, which, of course, lured the most vulnerable people to him, the ones who needed to borrow money to fuel their vice. It allowed him to get better odds, leading to more profit—if he managed to collect.

"How did you know Carl was involved?" I asked.

"His shop was the payment center. Whenever you'd have money to give to Greg, you'd go in there, and you'd tell Carl you wanted to buy a copy of *Finnegan's Wake*, since Carl believed no one in their right mind would ever actually buy that book, let alone read it."

I let out a snort. I had always thought James Joyce was an overrated writer who had capitalized on the women around him capitulating to make his life as easy as possible so he could write nonsense and pretend it was the greatest work ever known to man. Maybe there was more to this whole genetics thing than I thought.

"Anyway, when you'd tell him that, Carl would tell you he hadn't got any copies in stock, but he could order some in, and he'd ask if you wanted to pay in advance. You'd say yes, and he'd hand over a slip of paper, where you'd write your name and phone number and hand it back to him with the money. And he'd thank you and tell you he'd give you a call when the book arrived."

"What about after..." Maggie's voice trailed off, and I realized how difficult this conversation must have been for her.

Norman did too, because he answered quickly. "Erm, well, it was so quick, once we found out Carl was sick. There was no real plan put in place. Carl's illness was just so sudden."

Maggie nodded. "Right. All right."

"I'm real sorry, Maggie. I know Carl meant the world to you."

"Thank you, Norman. Now, can we ask where you were this morning, around nine?"

"Out here," Norman replied. "Been out working since just after six."

"Did anyone see you?" I asked.

"Only the cows."

"What about the night Greg was killed?"

"Sure, I was in town that night. Drinking at Puddle and Boot. Ask around there. They'll remember me. Not sure how I got home, but I woke up in me bed the next morning." Norman let out a loud chuckle at his own joke that made his belly bounce up and down slightly, and he held it in place with his hand. "But I'm telling you, I didn't kill Greg. I had his money. And I've had much worse debts than that which I've got out from under. Ten grand wasn't going to make or break me. I certainly wouldn't kill over that amount of money. I own this bloody farm, and with the way prices have soared since half of London decided they want to retire or buy a second home in Cornwall, I'd be set for life if I just sold it off. I wasn't going to, but believe me, I wasn't going to take a man's life for so little."

I had to admit, it made sense.

"All right. Thanks for the help, Norman," Maggie said. "I'm guessing you don't know who killed Greg or can lead us in the right direction?"

He shook his head. "Sorry. You know what Greg was like. Fingers in the least savory of pies. I imagine there must be more people in Cornwall who wanted Greg dead than there are flies on the cows over there."

"I just have one more question," I asked. "You say Greg was working with Carl to launder the money through his store. But what about in his other business dealings? Do you know if they were working together otherwise?"

Norman frowned for a moment as he considered the question. "You know, I'm not really sure. I didn't know Greg as a friend. Our relationship was strictly business. It's possible, but he never did mention it to me."

"Okay, thanks."

We left Norman to go back into his shed while Maggie and I walked back to the car.

"Oh, no," I said when Maggie approached the driver's side door. "Not a chance. Hand those keys over. There's no way in hell I'm letting you drive back to town. Not after I nearly met God on the way here."

"You've never driven on this side of the road," Maggie argued.

"*You* weren't even driving on the correct side of the road half the time on the way up here," I shot back.

"My car, my rules. Do you want to walk back?"

"I want to drive."

"You don't have a license."

"I genuinely don't believe you do, either."

"Would you like to see mine? Would that help?"

"No, because you probably got it back when cars were still turned on with a crank at the front and topped out at ten miles an hour."

"Well, now, you're *definitely* not allowed to drive back. Are you getting in or not?"

I sighed and walked to the passenger side,

resigning myself to my fate. I certainly wasn't going to walk back from here; it would take hours.

Maggie sped back to town—literally—and when we finally came to a stop in her parking spot, I stepped out of the car and got down on my hands and knees, pretending to kiss the ground.

"I swear, you didn't get all of these dramatics from *my* side of the family," Maggie said, rolling her eyes.

"As long as I didn't get your driving skills, either," I shot back. "Now, since we're finally out of that death trap, what did you think of Norman? Think he's telling the truth?"

Maggie pursed her lips. "I'd like to think so. He's right, you know. Ten grand, to someone who owns a farm that size, it's not really what you'd kill over. He could have pulled equity out of the farm."

"How long has he had the property?"

"Since his parents passed away. Back in the late eighties. And it had already been paid off back then. You used to be able to buy a plot of land in this duchy for a reasonable price. Of course, that's not been the case for a few decades now, but it means those of us who have lived here forever have a bit of value in our homes. Someone like Norman could pull ten grand out with the bank easily to repay Greg. I think he had it right when he said it wasn't a large enough amount of money to be worth killing someone over."

I nodded. "Okay. Well, at least we're slowly making our way through this list. And I think it also narrows down our list of suspects: it was probably someone involved in this gambling thing. After all, Greg was killed in the bookstore, where the customers would go to make their payments. My bet is someone who owed Greg money told him to meet them at the bookstore to make the payment. After all, Carl was no longer there, they wouldn't have been seen, and there wouldn't have been any chance someone else would have walked in on them. It's the perfect place to make a drop-off."

"In fact, I wonder if Greg wasn't secretly using it that way for his own purposes," Maggie continued. "If Carl gave him a key, then all he had to worry about was me. And Greg wouldn't have thought an old woman like me would have had any interest in visiting the bookshop. Certainly not in the middle of the night. Everyone in town correctly assumed I wanted nothing to do with the place. I have no interest in running the store, and I made no secret of that."

"It makes perfect sense, then."

"We simply need to find the rest of the people on that list and find out which of them might have killed him."

"Great. I'm going to go back to the bookstore for now and get started with the painting. You know most of the people on that list, right? Can you organize who we're going to meet and when?"

"Yes, I can cover that. I'll also see if I can find out who Kevin might be."

"What do I do if I want to throw out some stuff from the bookstore? There are way too many shelves in there right now. I want it to be more open, but I don't know how I'm going to throw it all out."

"I'll call Robbie for you. He runs a skip hire and can put one just outside the shop in the alley. You fill it up, then give him a call when you're ready to have him take it away."

"Oh, that's cool. Thanks."

"Robbie's a good one. It's a bit late for today, but I can call him tomorrow morning, and he'll have you set up within a couple hours."

"Wow, even better. Great. In that case, text me if you manage to set up a meeting with someone. But until then, I'll be working."

I HEADED DOWN TO THE BOOKSTORE AND surveyed the space. I wanted to get rid of all the bookshelves in the middle of the room. There were too many of them, and they were too tall. They made this space look small and uninviting.

There were built-in bookcases along three of

the four walls. I was going to keep those and use them for the bulk of the books. I would paint the walls around them and the wall that faced the front, with the large window. I would paint the ceiling, too. Right now, it was black, matching the rest of the store. I would paint everything except the exposed beams; those would stay dark. Perfect.

With my plan in place, I walked to Wattle's, the hardware store, and bought some painting equipment, drop cloths, screwdrivers, and a hammer. Then I set about getting to work.

First, I moved all of the books I could into the small storage room at the back. I didn't want them around while I had the paint out. That took about an hour, loading pile after pile into a large cardboard box I'd found and doing trip after trip. I was going to have arms Arnold Schwarzenegger would be proud of after this.

When the room was empty of books, I decided to tackle the ceiling first. After all, I could stand on the now-empty bookshelves to get closer to it and make my job just a little bit easier.

I tested my theory first, carefully climbing up the shelves like a ladder, and when I confirmed that I was not only capable of getting up and down that way but that they would hold my weight, I pried open one of the tins of paint, poured a whole bunch into the paint tray, and got to work.

It took about forty minutes for me to paint the whole ceiling and the front wall of the store. Looking at the side of a can, I saw that this was a quick-drying type of paint, meaning I only had to wait an hour before I could do the second coat.

I spent that time disassembling two of the bookshelves and moving the pieces of wood toward the door. I put a quick ad up on Facebook Marketplace to see if anyone wanted them, but I knew there was likely to be no interest. The bookshelves Carl had bought were large, tall, and deep. They weren't the most versatile in the world, and I had a sneaking suspicion I wasn't going to get a lot of bites from my ad.

Still, if there was someone out there who could use them, I was willing to try, so as I dismantled them, I carefully kept track of what pieces belonged to what shelf.

After an hour passed, I started on my second coat of paint. I did the ceiling then moved the paint to the floor, where I could finish up along the wall.

I was about three-quarters of the way through when, out of the corner of my eye, I saw something falling next to me.

"What the—" I started, instinctively taking a step back. The item plummeted to the ground, landing in the middle of the tray of paint, splashing it everywhere. And then, as if that wasn't surprising enough, it let out a squeal, jumped out and began running across the floor.

"Don't tell me this place is haunted too," I muttered to myself. But no. Ghosts didn't leave footprints behind as they ran all along the floor of the bookstore, darting between the bookshelves that still hadn't been disassembled.

And if they did, those footprints probably wouldn't be kitten shaped.

Chapter 17

"Where on earth did you come from?" I asked the cat as I darted after it, following the trail like Dorothy on the yellow brick road. Or more accurately, the white paint, cat-paw-decorated road. The kitten scampered around the room, leaving messy white footprints along the wooden floor, which was so dark it was nearly black.

The footprints got lighter and lighter, but before they could disappear completely, I caught my intruder.

"Got you," I said as I scooped him up. He let out a mewl of dissatisfaction as he squirmed in my hand, but I kept a firm grip on him and had a look.

He was young, obviously. Just a kitten. I'd never had a pet before, so I wasn't sure exactly how old he was, but he was little. He couldn't have been more than a few months old.

"Where did you even come from?" I asked, looking up at the ceiling. There was an old heating vent that came out right where he'd popped out from. He must have gotten in there somehow. "Okay, well, let's get you cleaned up."

The kitten let out another mewl, as if he understood me. I took him back to the small bathroom, grateful that there was soap next to the sink. I turned on the water, waited for it to get lukewarm, then began washing the paint off the kitten, who made his displeasure at the whole situation very loudly known.

"Do you want me to leave you like this? With all this paint on you? Trust me, buddy, it's for your own good," I scolded him.

The water that ran down the drain started off practically opaque but slowly lightened until eventually, it ran completely clear. Confident that the kitten was now paint free, I grabbed the small hand towel off the hook near the door. It was pristine, which told me it had never been used—gross—but it meant I was able to dry off the kitten before snugly wrapping him up in a purrito.

Finally, I got a good look at him. Or her. Either way, kitty was absolutely gorgeous. And loud. His squeals pierced the air as he complained about being trapped, but after a minute or so, he seemed to realize that he was now dry and comfortable, and he stopped.

He was a calico, with absolutely gorgeous

markings. His orange and black face made him look like a tiger, and he was dotted with specs of white. His yellow-green eyes locked with mine, curiosity etched all over his face.

"Where did you come from, buddy?" I asked, carrying him back into the main part of the store. I walked back to where the paint was and looked up. Sure enough, he had to have fallen out of the old vent that emerged from the ceiling right above where I'd kept the paint.

It looked like my plans were on hold for a little bit; I had to find this guy some food and see if anyone knew where he had come from.

I locked up the store and walked down the street to the Ugly Mug Café. I figured if nothing else, Sophie could give me some milk to feed the little guy while I figured out what to do with him.

As soon as I walked in, I held my little purrito boy up to the sky, like he was Simba in *The Lion King*.

Sophie's face lit up as she let out a squeal. "Is that what I think it is?"

"If you think it's a tiny feline intruder causing chaos and adorable vandalism in the bookstore, you'd be right."

Sophie immediately darted out from behind the counter to have a look. "Oh, she's so adorable. What a sweetheart."

"She?"

"Yeah, she's a tortoiseshell and white. Almost

every single tortie cat in the world is female. Something about how their genetics work."

"Huh, go figure. I never knew that. She fell out of the ceiling vent and into a tub of paint. Then she ran around the store, leaving footprints everywhere. I got her cleaned up, which is why she looks like she wants to murder me. She just had a bath and that's why she's in the purrito. But I figured maybe you'd be able to give me some milk for her."

"You've never had cats, have you?" Sophie asked with a bemused smile.

"No. Why?"

"They're lactose intolerant. You can't give them milk despite the stereotype. Well, you *can*, but it's not good for them. You need kitten meal replacement or some kitten food. She looks just old enough that you should be able to wean her and get her onto some wet food pretty easily."

I looked at the cat curiously. "What do you think? Are you ready for some wet food?"

She let out a meow in reply.

"I think that was a yes," Sophie said.

"I have no idea what I'm going to do with her. I guess I should look for her mom and siblings."

"You can, yes. But I think you've just discovered the universal cat distribution system, babes."

"The what?"

"The universal cat distribution system. Basically, when the universe deems it time for you to have a cat, one will appear fully formed, seemingly out of nowhere. That's obviously what's happened here."

I raised my eyebrows. "Not only does that sound ridiculous, but I can barely keep myself alive right now, let alone this little thing. I don't think the universe thinks it's time for me to have a cat."

Sophie shrugged. "I don't make the rules. That's how it works. Congratulations! You have a new kitty. Now, let me see if I can get her a little something while you run down to the pet shop to grab some essentials."

"What do I need?"

"Cans of wet food specifically formulated for kittens. If you can find one that's for both kittens and feeding mothers, even better. You need a litterbox, a scoop, a carrying crate, and some litter. Bowls for her to eat and drink from. Those are the basics. Then, of course, there's toys. She'll love a feather teaser, and you'll want a scratching post or two. What does Maggie think of her?"

"I, uh, may not have told her about the kitten just yet. You were my first stop."

Sophie grinned. "I'm sure she'll love her. Okay, leave the kitten with me; I'll make sure she gets some nutrition into her. There's some chicken in the back that's going into the sandwiches. I can cut some of that up into tiny bits."

"Thanks, Sophie," I said gratefully. "I'll be back soon."

I left the coffee shop and immediately plugged "pet shop" into my Google Maps app. Armed with my list of items to purchase, I headed over there, only to see the lights out and a sign on the front reading "Closed—family emergency, sorry! Be back tomorrow."

"Damn it," I muttered to myself. Well, there was always a grocery store. They should have at least the basics. I typed that into the search bar and found there was one only a few streets away. Perfect. I headed that way, mentally going through the list of what I needed in my head.

This morning, someone had tried to kill me, and this afternoon, I had a kitten. At least for now. I was going to try and find her mother and any siblings she might have had. I didn't quite believe in the thing Sophie had mentioned, the universal cat distribution system.

I found the grocery store easily, and soon after I entered, a man greeted me. Middle-aged, with graying brown hair, he had one of those faces that could easily melt into a crowd. Nothing especially stood out; he was average in every way.

"Hello. Can I help you find anything?" The name badge on his light-blue button-up shirt read "Jerome – Owner," and I knew that was familiar from somewhere but couldn't quite place it.

"Yes, please," I said with a smile. "I'm looking for pet supplies. A cat, specifically."

"Of course. Right this way."

As I followed him past the fresh produce, it clicked. Jerome Woods was one of our suspects, one of the people Maggie thought was an entry in Greg's book. How much money did Jerome owe Greg? I couldn't quite remember.

"Thank you so much. I'm new in town, and I think I might have happened upon a new kitten. The pet shop is closed—family emergency."

Jerome nodded. "Yes, I spoke to Harriet this morning. Her daughter's appendix burst, and she's gone into surgery in London. Harriet wanted to be there, obviously, when she wakes up."

"Oh no."

"I'm sure she'll be fine, but as a result, Harriet's closed up shop for the day. You said you're new in town? You wouldn't happen to be Carl Summers's daughter, would you? I heard she arrived the other day."

"That's me," I said, flashing a smile. "I'm planning on reopening the bookstore once I've got everything sorted out and settled in. Although Gregory Hamlisch's death hasn't helped, since that's where the body was found."

Jerome shook his head. "I always knew that man's lifestyle was going to catch up to him one day. He was always involved in something shady.

I'm sorry you got dragged into all of it, though."

"Thanks. I have to admit, it's not how I planned on starting my new life here."

"Of course."

"I heard Greg was running some sort of gambling ring. He would loan people money if they wanted to make bets because you can't do it online with credit cards anymore."

Jerome shook his head. "I'm afraid I don't know anything about that."

I knew he was lying, but I didn't want to push the man while he was openly giving me information. "Well, I'm sure the police will get to the bottom of this. By the way, when does this store open in the mornings?"

"Eight o'clock," Jerome replied. "I'm here every day, from eight until five, if you need anything. Except Sundays, when we're closed."

"Are you very busy in the mornings?"

"Quite a bit, yes. A lot of the older people prefer to come in around then. Usually, we're quite busy until around ten o'clock, then it quietens down until the middle of the afternoon and picks up again. Here's our pet section. Can I help you find anything specific?"

"No, thanks. I'm just going to have a look and see what I can grab. Thanks for the help."

"Not a problem. And welcome to town. I hope the shadow cast by Greg's death doesn't cause you too much consternation."

"Thanks. I know the police consider me a suspect, but I'm hoping they'll find the real killer soon."

Jerome snorted. "Of all the people in this town who might have wanted Greg dead, I'm sure a newcomer is last on the list. He made enough enemies. Don't you worry. It will all be fine."

Giving me a reassuring nod, Jerome left, and I pulled out my phone to send Maggie a quick text. *Just met Jerome. Didn't admit to anything to do with gambling, but I didn't push him. He was here this morning, though, it sounds like.*

Of course, it was always possible that Jerome could have left the grocery store and gone out to follow me. But how would he have known where I was? I hadn't walked past this store on the way to the trails. How would he have known we were investigating? No, it didn't make any sense for Jerome to be the killer. I silently crossed him off the suspect list and focused on the cat supplies.

Ten minutes later, I had everything I needed and was walking out with a full bag over my shoulder. I returned to the Ugly Mug Café, where Sophie had abandoned her post at the counter and was entertaining a couple of customers with the kitten at one of the tables. I supposed she was going to need a name sooner rather than later.

As soon as she saw me, Sophie waved me

over. "Have you got everything for her? She's a total sweetheart."

I smiled when my eyes landed on the kitten once more, and as soon as she saw me, she scampered over, jumped up onto my arm, and started climbing up my jacket until she reached my shoulder.

"See? She's yours. Universal cat distribution system at work," Sophie said confidently.

"What are you calling her?" one of the customers asked.

"I'm not sure yet. I've never had a pet before. I've never had to name one."

"The thing with cats is it doesn't matter," the other customer said. "They don't care what their names are, and they're not going to listen to you when you call them, so you can be as creative as you want."

I laughed. "Good to know. Okay, I'm going to take her back to the bookshop with me, get her settled in, see if I can find her mom or siblings."

I scooped the kitten back up off the table, said goodbye to Sophie and the customers, then headed back out into the afternoon.

It wasn't until I reached the bookstore front door that I realized I should have ordered another slice of that cheesecake while I was at the coffee shop. "You really have a hold on me," I said to the kitten, who remained sitting on my shoulder while I carried everything. "Imagine being so adorable you make me forget about cheesecake."

The kitten let out another little meow as if telling me, "Of course I'm that cute," and I laughed while I unlocked the front door once more.

Chapter 18

When I got back to the bookstore, Maggie replied to my text.

That's one more down, I suppose. I would have thought Jerome could have been a good suspect. I wouldn't have put it past Greg to threaten to make it known that Jerome was gambling. In a small community like this, he would have wanted to keep that to himself.

Yeah. But it doesn't make any sense. If you can go over there and find out from one of the other workers if they saw him around nine, nine thirty, that would seal it. But even if he found out through the local grapevine that we were investigating, how could he have known where I was? I didn't walk past the grocery store this morning. And he wasn't in the Ugly Mug while I was ordering my breakfast.

I sent the text, paused, then quickly added another. *PS. How do you feel about cats?*

While I waited for Maggie to answer, I put the stuff I'd bought down on the ground. The

221

kitten immediately began investigating the insides of the bags.

"You're a curious little thing, aren't you?" I asked her.

She looked up at me, tilting her head to the side.

"What's your name? Where's your family? Where did you come from? You can't have just appeared out of nowhere, as much as Sophie says that's how it works. Let's get you some food then try and find your family."

I pried open a can of wet food and placed it on a small paper plate. I'd bought a pack of them since the grocery store didn't have any cat food bowls.

The kitten immediately dove in and began munching away. She was a loud eater, constantly making noise while she buried her head in the food.

I laughed at the sight. "Weirdo."

While she did that, I began pushing one of the bookshelves toward the front of the room. Without any books on them, they were light enough that I just managed to do it. Then I climbed on top with my phone and poked it up into the vent with the video on, trying to see if there was anything in there.

To my dismay, it didn't seem that there was. No other kittens. No momma cat.

Just the little ball of fluff who looked up at me, her face covered in wet food.

"That's how I look when I come back from an all-you-can-eat buffet too. Don't worry," I said to the kitten.

She let out a meow then buried her face back into the food once more.

I turned on my phone's flashlight and had another look in the vent, but no. There was no sign of any other cats.

"Well, I guess you're mine, then. Unless we find your family somewhere else. Maybe Sophie was right about the whole 'universe dropping off a cat' thing."

I climbed down off the bookshelf and set about getting everything ready for the kitten. I got the litterbox, googled how much litter to put in it, filled it up, then had a look around.

The floor was covered in cat-painted foot-prints. They started near the window where I'd been painting and continued through the whole store, curling around where the bookshelves were, until they reached the counter.

Funnily enough, I liked them. I was going to have to buy some sort of sealant, because I was totally keeping them. They added a little bit of fun and whimsy to this place, which was exactly the kind of feeling I was going for.

"Thanks for the décor help, kiddo," I said to the kitten.

My phone binged again, and I read the response from Maggie.

You're right, it doesn't make sense. I've hunted down

a Kevin MacMillan. He's a young man, works at the local butcher. From what I've heard, he's always asking about ways to make some more money, so a likely gambler. We can go see him tomorrow. As for cats, I've had a few in my life.

I snapped a picture of the kitten and sent it to Maggie with a caption. *Good, because this little bundle of joy dropped into my life—quite literally—and I'm growing attached. She loves food as much as I do. Sounds like a plan re: Kevin.*

Maggie's reply came through a moment later. *That's how they get you, kittens. They look adorable, and you bring them into your home, and by the time you realize all they do is eat and commit crimes, they've wormed their way into your heart.*

I can't imagine a better life than eating and committing crime. Anyway, I'll be bringing her home with me once I'm done here. I haven't named her yet. I'll be back in a few hours.

While I had the phone out, I also sent a message to Ada. *I think I've figured out why the crime took place at the bookstore. Apparently, my dad was working with Greg to launder the money and make it clean. I think when he died, Greg figured he might as well keep using the bookstore as a meeting place, especially in the middle of the night when only my grandmother had keys. He correctly assumed she wasn't going to interrupt a visit.*

When I opened Facebook Messenger, I was surprised to find I had two responses to my ad. The first was someone who just wanted a single bookcase. I sent him the address and told him to come by in the next couple of hours.

The second wanted as many as I was willing to give, so I repeated the message and set about dismantling them so they could be more easily transported.

The kitten spent the whole time moving between her food bowl and checking out what I was doing. When I hunched over, she would jump onto my back and climb up onto my shoulder to get a better look. She chased errant screws around on the ground and generally caused chaos.

As Maggie had said, committing crimes and eating.

The first man came over and picked up a bookcase about an hour later. He told me he'd been looking for something to keep his model airplanes on and that this would do the trick nicely. The other man arrived twenty minutes after that and gave me a hand disassembling the rest. Next thing I knew, all the freestanding bookcases in the store were gone.

When the second man left, with all the bookcases and screws to go with them safely in his truck, I took a deep breath and looked around. The space looked way, way bigger already. I could see the entire store now. Standing in the entrance, I surveyed three walls with empty bookcases, floor to ceiling. The counter was to the left, and next to me was the huge, open window that let in so much light. The floor was still in great shape, and the little kitten footprints definitely added to the atmosphere. This was what I wanted.

I could easily fit hundreds of books on the three shelves that were already here, and I could focus on making the rest of the space as welcoming as possible for people.

My phone binged, and I pulled it out to find a response from Ada. *That's an answer, at least. Although I suppose it doesn't get you closer to the killer, beyond telling you the gambling side is probably the one to focus on.*

That's what I was thinking too. We're going to interview a couple more people tomorrow and see what we can find out. We eliminated a few more suspects. Oh, by the way, you wouldn't happen to know a Kevin MacMillan, would you? Works at the butcher shop?

Sorry, no. I don't really know a lot of people in town. I haven't lived here long enough.

Cool. No worries. Hey, do you want to meet up, and I can buy you a coffee or something? I owe you for this morning.

You don't, but I'd love to.

We texted back and forth a bit and eventually agreed to meet tomorrow for lunch at the Ugly Mug Café.

I then went to the counter. The police had taken the computer but left everything else alone. Good. I was going to need everything I could to find out how a bookstore actually ran. I had no idea where Carl had ordered his books from, how to accept payments, and about a thousand more things that I would have to figure out before I was ready to open. That was the plan for tonight.

I found an old cloth bag in the back of the store, so I threw in all of the kitten's things, as well as the papers I'd found on the counter, and we headed home. I'd made a lot of progress today, at least on the bookstore.

Frustratingly, I didn't think we were any closer to finding the killer. It was unlikely to be Jerome, and I didn't think Norman had done it, but we still didn't know who had killed Greg.

I WALKED HOME, THE KITTEN IN MY ARMS, AND as soon as I entered the front door, Maggie poked her head out from the kitchen.

"All right, let's have a look at the little ball of chaos you've brought," she said.

As if understanding her words, the kitten jumped out of my arms and let out a loud meow. She was so young the sound was more of a squeal.

"She says you're rude," I told her.

"Tell her as long as she doesn't pay rent, I'm allowed to be."

"Sorry, kiddo," I said to the cat. "You're just going to have to put up with it."

"What have you named her?"

I shrugged. "Haven't decided yet. But she's cute. How about Slightly Burned Toast? We can call her Toast for short."

Maggie nodded. "I like it."

"What do you think, Toast?" I asked the kitten.

She let out another meow.

"I think she likes it."

I spent a while unpacking her things while Maggie set about making dinner for the two of us. I pulled out all of the papers I'd grabbed from Carl's store and set them on the table.

"Do you mind if I keep these out?" I asked Maggie. "I'll take them to my room if you find it too painful."

She shook her head. "No, it's all right."

I paused. "I'm sorry you had to find out about what he was up to today. With Greg, I mean."

Maggie gave me a curt nod but didn't meet my eye. "Thank you. I always knew Carl marched to the beat of his own drum. And I knew he was always looking for something. Something he didn't find. I never thought he would turn to crime, though. I knew the bookstore wasn't doing as well as he wanted it to. But still. That he would go into business with Dirk Evers and launder money for him…"

"He made a mistake," I said. "That doesn't make him a bad person."

228

Maggie looked at me. "I'm not one of those people who thinks everything in the criminal code is correct and should be adhered to."

"I noticed, given the way you drive," I replied dryly.

She cracked a small smile at that. "I may have technically broken a few laws in my day. If there's one thing I've learned in my time on this earth, it's that nothing is black and white. We're taught to know our right from our wrong and we're instilled with this notion that in order to be good people, we must firmly stick to the side of what the government has deemed to be objectively right.

"But it's never that simple. The law is inflexible, to the point of detriment in many situations. I tried my best to teach Carl right from wrong, in a real-world sense, but laundering money from an illegal gambling operation? That's beyond what I believe is right, and I think Carl would have known that as well. And while it's one thing to be disappointed in your child, it impacts a person differently when that child has recently passed."

I reached across the table and took Maggie's hand in mine. "I'm sorry. I really am."

"It would be different if I could confront him about it. Ask him what he thought he was doing. But at the same time, Carl was a grown man. He was in his forties. He should have known better. There comes a time when a mother has to let her children make their own mistakes, and this was a mistake. But I wish I could have asked him about it."

"Yeah," I said quietly.

"It makes no difference in the end. At least as far as I know, he wasn't involved in anything violent."

"There is that."

"Let me know what you find in those papers, would you? If you have any information on how the store was doing?"

"I will. I'm not sure how much I'm going to find here, though. The police took the computer away, going by the marks on the counter. I imagine most of the data will be on there."

Maggie shook her head. "Carl wasn't much of a technology buff. There's a good chance you've got all the information you need in there. And even if he had used the computer, he would have printed out a hard copy. He didn't trust hard drives. Said those things failed all the time."

"Oh, good. In that case, I'll see what I can find out."

While Maggie returned to the kitchen to continue dinner, I sorted through all of the documents I'd grabbed from the desk. I pulled out an empty notepad and began writing down anything important.

One of the first things I found was an invoice from a distributor. I took down all of their contact information and Carl's account number and made a note to call them first thing tomorrow. I was going to need to get set up with them myself.

Next, I found financial documents. I had majored in marketing in college, but it still meant I'd had to take a number of general business courses, including accounting. I could read income statements and balance sheets, and it quickly became obvious that my father had been in the red. Until he went into business with Dirk Evers, at which point his income rose significantly.

"I think this explains why he went into business with Greg," I explained. "Carl was bleeding money with the bookstore. Where did he get the money to set it up?"

"His job as a lawyer in the City. He made a very good living, but he wasn't happy. The home he had bought rose in value significantly when he lived in it. It allowed him to purchase the land the bookshop sat on as well as this house."

I nodded. "But he must have decided he needed a bit more to tide him over while he got the place up and running."

Maggie shook her head. "It's so disappointing. He wanted to be successful as an entrepreneur, but frankly, he just didn't have the skills. He was an excellent lawyer. He should have simply opened up shop here as a solicitor."

"Sometimes, we don't realize until we follow

our dreams that they were actually nightmares," I said quietly.

"Isn't that the truth?"

"Okay. Well, that explains a lot. And frankly, I don't think this is a lost cause. A ton of the money he spent was on stock, which I don't have to pay for. I'm getting some furniture for cheap or free. Do you mind if I borrow your car to go pick it up?"

Maggie narrowed her eyes at me. "You dent it, you bought it."

"Fine with me."

We ate spaghetti Bolognese with garlic bread while I pored over the rest of the documents. Toast quickly found that she liked sitting on the arm of the sofa, where she promptly fell asleep.

"I won't need any trash removed, either," I said to Maggie. "I managed to palm off all the bookshelves to other people in town."

"Oh, good. That will save you a bit of money. How are you doing for cash?"

I shrugged. "I have some savings. I've always been frugal. Given as I'm not paying rent anymore, it should last me a while. The store shouldn't be too expensive to run right off the bat, either. Carl had a ton of books in stock. I'll need to buy some others to really give the vibe that I want and bring people in, but I think I can probably last a year without making a profit. And I'd like to do it within six months."

Maggie nodded. "Smart. Have you come up with a name?"

"I was thinking The Broken Spine. It's kind of creepy, kind of cool, and there are now some mysterious paw prints on the floor that add to the cool vibe."

"The Broken Spine." Maggie tried the words on then gave me a curt nod. "Good. Clever. Has some kick to it. I like it."

"Glad you approve. It's all coming together. Now we just need to find the killer."

"We will go speak with Kevin tomorrow. And Dennis Grigg. In fact, we will hire him to move all of the furniture you've got planned. That will give us an excellent excuse to speak to him."

"Sounds like a plan."

"If all goes well, by tomorrow afternoon, we will hopefully have narrowed down which one of them is the killer."

"I hope so."

Chapter 19

THE NEXT MORNING, I WOKE UP TO TOAST standing on my chest, staring intently at my face as she let out the loudest meow she could.

I yawned and grabbed at the nightstand until my hand landed on my phone. I tapped the screen to see that it was just after five in the morning. I was pretty sure. The cracks made it hard to see the exact time.

"Really?" I muttered, flinging my head back onto the pillow. "It's not even five in the morning."

Meow.

On the bright side, while I was approaching something resembling a normal sleep schedule, I still wasn't completely over the jet lag yet, so a five o'clock wake-up call to feed the ball of chaos on my bed wasn't the worst thing in the world. I still grumbled a little bit at her as I crawled out of bed and threw on some clothes before heading downstairs and opening a new tin of cat food for her.

Toast immediately dug in. She wasn't having any problems eating the wet food, so I supposed there was no need for any milk replacement. Still, when she came up for air, her whole little face was covered in the paté, and I let out an involuntary giggle.

"You eat like a toddler," I admonished her, heading to the kitchen to grab a cloth with which to wipe her face. Toast wasn't a fan of getting cleaned up, but once I was finished, she hopped up onto my lap and started purring contentedly.

Pulling out my laptop, I made up a new list of things I had to do for the bookstore. By the time seven o'clock rolled around, I left Toast sleeping on the arm of the couch—now that she'd successfully woken me up at an ungodly hour so that she could eat, apparently it was time for her to enjoy some much-deserved sleep—and I headed down to the Ugly Mug Café.

"How's the kitten?" were the first words out of Sophie's mouth when I entered.

"Woke me up just before five for food."

She barked out a laugh. "That sounds about right. Have you named her yet?"

"Slightly Burned Toast. Toast for short."

"Great name. I approve."

"Thanks. She's pleased with her wet food. Buries her face in it and makes this strange sound when she's eating, like she's trying to meow while inhaling food."

"Cats are basically just small weirdos. Make sure you get her lots of stuff to scratch, and she'll probably leave your furniture alone."

"Good call. I'll check out the pet store later. Hey, you said you're an artist, right?"

Sophie nodded. "Yeah."

"Can I hire you to paint the sign outside of the bookstore? I've settled on a name. The Broken Spine."

"Ooh, I like that. Of course. I'd be thrilled to help. What kind of lettering are you thinking?"

"I want something that really says England, you know? I was thinking plain, serif lettering. Since the exterior is painted dark blue, I was thinking gold would stand out well."

"Perfect. I'll take care of it," Sophie said. "I'll make it look amazing."

"Thanks so much. Now, while I'm here, I definitely need a coffee. And a pastry. You know, for energy."

"Can't solve crime if you haven't got energy," Sophie agreed.

"I'll be back here for lunch today, too. I'm meeting a friend. Hey, you know Aksel? Private investigator, used to be a cop, we were chatting about him the other day?"

"Sure. Why?"

"What's the deal with him? He's investigating this case, supposedly."

Sophie's eyebrows rose skyward. "Supposedly? You were saying yesterday he was investigating for sure. What's going on?"

"Well, the first time we came across him was at Greg's home, although I will literally chop my own finger off before I admit to having been there if you tell anyone."

"Understood."

"He said he was investigating the case too, although he wouldn't tell me who hired him."

"Okay. A bit sketchy but also understandable."

"Right. Until yesterday, when I went out onto the trails you suggested, and someone tried to kill me."

Sophie brought a hand to her mouth. "What? Are you serious right now, babes?"

"Yeah. I went down to one of the beaches and found a path back up via the rocks along the cliff."

"I think I know the one. Past the little caves on the far side of the beach?"

"That sounds like the one."

"That's a really common path for locals to use to get back up. It's quite safe, normally, as long as you stay on the track."

"And I was safe—until someone shoved me from behind, off the rocks and into the water."

Sophie gasped. "That's so dangerous."

"Yeah. I almost died, and I'm not even exaggerating. Whoever pushed me off wanted to kill me. Luckily, Ada saved me. She's the friend I'm meeting later. Anyway, we were walking back toward town when we ran into Aksel."

"Okay, that's *really* sketchy."

"That's what we both thought too."

"What do you think he was doing? Trying to see if he succeeded in killing you? But surely, if he was just investigating the case separately, he wouldn't have wanted you out of the way."

"No, I agree. That would be beyond psychopathic behavior. I think if Aksel tried to kill me, it means he's the one who also killed Greg."

"That makes total sense. Wow. Okay, what do I know about him? He used to be a policeman here in town."

I nodded. "I've heard that."

"A couple of years ago, he left suddenly. I heard there was some sort of internal scandal inside the police force. It was all very hush-hush. About five people left around then, including some higher-ranking officials. And Aksel."

"Do you know what it was about?"

"Not exactly. The details were never revealed, but I did overhear some officers talking about it back then when they were waiting for their coffee. I think there was some sort of corruption scandal. I don't know the details."

"I wonder if Aksel was involved, and that's why he quit along with the others," I said darkly.

"It's possible. He quit, but he never left town. I did know he'd pivoted career-wise and became a private investigator, but I don't know much beyond that. Believe me, for a while a few years ago, it was all anyone was talking about. And there were rumors."

"What kind?"

"Some people claimed that some of the members of the police here had got involved in the running of drugs and that they were conveniently looking the other way while certain boats returned to harbor with their loads and that in exchange, the officers involved were receiving payoffs."

"Okay. That's always a pretty standard accusation when people think the police are corrupt."

"It is. There was also a rumor that evidence in some drug cases had mysteriously gone missing and that the only people who could have stolen the evidence were other police officers."

"And I'm guessing in these cases, the evidence just happened to be giant bricks of coke."

"Something like that, yes. I also heard one of the superintendents had been caught deleting records of arrest files from people he had taken bribes from."

I raised my eyebrows. "That would be something."

"So as you can see, there were a lot of different rumors flying around. No one knows for sure what happened, as far as I can tell. I certainly don't know whose stories were fact, whose were fiction, and I wouldn't even be surprised if they were all fake. In a small town like this, rumors almost take on a life of their own sometimes. You can't trust what people say, especially when there's no evidence. So what I do know is that Aksel was part of the group of officers who left after the scandal, but I don't know exactly why he did."

"It's suspicious as hell, though."

"It is," Sophie agreed. "Everyone knows *something* happened, but the police closed ranks and kept the details to themselves."

"Good to know. So yeah, now you've got the whole story. I don't trust Aksel one bit. I think he could very well be the killer. The only question is, why would he have met with Greg that night, in the bookstore? I don't have an answer for that. It makes more sense that Greg would have been using it to meet the gamblers and exchanging money there, and we have no sign that Aksel was someone who was gambling with Greg."

Sophie pursed her lips. "I'm afraid I don't know. What I can tell you, though, is that you've got a lot of support here in town."

"Oh?"

"Word's got around that the police suspect you and Maggie. From everything I've heard, people are outraged that the police would treat a total newcomer to town like this, especially given Greg's history."

"That's a relief, at least."

"I thought you'd want to know. You'll hear people talk about how in Cornwall, people aren't welcoming. Well, that's a load of rubbish. Sure, we're not particularly polite to the Londoners who come down and buy their second or third home that they leave empty for fifty weeks a year, driving up prices so the rest of us can't afford a first, but ultimately, you'll never find a nicer group of people. We're a community, and as long as you don't break the cardinal rule, you're welcome here."

"What's the cardinal rule?"

Sophie grinned. "Jam before cream."

I laughed "Right, I learned that the other day."

"If you pick up only one habit from living here, let it be that one. Also, if you ever go to other parts of England and they tell you you're saying it wrong, you can tell them you're from Cornwall, where 'scone' rhymes with 'stone.'"

"Got it. Luckily, that one's normal to me. We say it that way in America too."

"I noticed."

"Actually, I haven't had a proper scone since I've come here. I'm a sucker for cheesecake."

"Let's remedy that right now," Sophie said, grabbing a plate. "I'll get you some Cornish clotted cream too. And strawberry jam. We get it made locally, and of course it's the perfect season for it."

"I love strawberry season."

"Best fruit in the world," Sophie agreed. "Okay, I'll bring that out to you. And a coffee?"

"Yes, please."

"Boris mug or something different?"

"Oh man, I love the Boris mug, but I feel like I need to truly sample the variety you have here. Give me something really cool. But still ugly."

"You got it. Do you still want that cheesecake too?"

"I'll grab it with lunch instead."

"Cool."

I paid for my items then took a seat by the window and let my eyes wander out onto the street while I waited. It was obviously going to be another gorgeous day. Looking up to the sky, I couldn't see a single cloud, and the triangular flags that draped the space between the buildings flapped gently in the soft morning breeze.

This was a good day to try and find a killer.

Sophie came by a minute later with a couple of scones and some cream and jam. When she put the mug of coffee down in front of me to go with it, I snorted.

"Okay, this one's really good too."

This mug had been designed to resemble a person's foot. I was going to have to drink from the ankle. But it wasn't just an ordinary foot-shaped mug, if there was such a thing. No, this had obviously been handcrafted to look incredibly realistic, with creases for the tendons, and knobbly toes. Six of them. It had been painted a light peachy color that wasn't unlike the shade of my own skin, and the toenails had each been given a manicure. Different, bright colors for each of the six toes, which spread apart in a way that made them almost look like they were wiggling.

"This mug creeped me out so much the first six months I worked here I refused to use it," Sophie replied.

"It looks like it's about to reach over and try to caress my hand."

"Right? It's so lifelike. I hate it. But I thought you would enjoy it. It was between this one and the mug that looks like a butt."

"Oh, I definitely want that one next."

"I'll make sure to note that down. Enjoy."

I carefully cut the first scone in half and added a teaspoon of the gorgeous red jam before topping it with a hefty helping of clotted cream. Taking a bite, I felt like I was going to melt into the chair. This was so good, it gave cheesecake a run for its money.

"I love it," I called out to Sophie at the counter.

"I knew you would," she replied.

Just then, the front door opened once more, and I turned to see none other than Aksel Evans walking in.

Chapter 20

I BRIEFLY CONSIDERED TRYING TO SLIP underneath the table like a plate of spaghetti thrown at the wall and slowly sliding back to the ground. But as soon as he walked in, Aksel's eyes scanned the room. And once they landed on me, he stopped.

Striding over, he sat down in the chair across from me. I tried to ignore the jolt in my chest as soon as my eyes landed on him. Sure, he was good-looking. His hair was tousled with that just-got-out-of-bed look, his eyes sparkled in a way that should be illegal before nine in the morning, and he sat down with the confidence of a man who walked streets paved with gold. But Aksel was about to find out that just because the fabric of his shirt strained just a little against his muscles didn't mean I was going to fawn all over him.

He might have been hot, but there was a good chance he'd tried to kill me yesterday.

"I didn't realize we had a date," I said dryly.

"You've been investigating Gregory Hamlisch's death, even after I warned you to stay away from the case. Even after someone nearly tried to kill you," Aksel growled. It wasn't a question; it was a statement. "I told you to stay away from it."

"Believe it or not, I'm not actually obligated to take advice from random men, especially when they look like they brush their hair with a balloon."

A slightly amused smile flittered over Aksel's lips. "But if I'd slicked my hair back like an accountant, it would be fine?"

"No. But you would look less ridiculous."

"I look great," Aksel replied with an unshakable confidence that annoyed me. He did look great, but he didn't have to be so blatant about acknowledging it. I was trying to insult him into leaving. It worked with most men. "Now, don't change the topic. You aren't an official part of this investigation."

"Neither are you," I pointed out.

"Wrong. I'm authorized to pursue this. It's my job."

"Authorized by who? Is that why the first time I ran into you was in the middle of the night in the victim's home? Because nothing screams authorization like breaking into a person's house."

Aksel pinched the bridge of his nose. "You don't know anything about me or my investigation."

"Likewise."

"I know you're not an official investigator. You showed up here a few days ago to claim your inheritance. You're a regular woman who arrived in town, found a body, and decided that you were going to play detective in your fun little adventure abroad without realizing that there would be consequences."

I leaned forward, narrowing my eyes at Aksel. "Believe me, I would love nothing more than to quietly go about my business and make a new life for myself here. But I can't. Because somebody decided to drop a body on the property that I own, and now, the police detectives with the IQ of a cardboard box working this case think I'm the killer. So I don't have a choice but to get to the bottom of this.

"Meanwhile, I wonder if you're not using your job as a cover. I find it awfully suspicious that you were at the beach the other day, right when someone tried to kill me. And now you're sitting there, trying to tell me to stay away from this case. Why's that? Because I'm too close to the truth? You're not the only one who's been out there asking questions.

"I know you used to be a cop. Why'd you

give it up? Because you were caught in a scandal and had no other choice?"

A flash of something crossed Aksel's face but was gone a split second later. I couldn't quite make out the emotion. Anger? Annoyance?

When he replied, he spoke carefully, as if he was considering every word. "You don't know anything about what happened with me and the police."

"And you don't know a thing about my life or who I am. You're the one who invited himself here when I was just trying to enjoy a couple of scones. You might not be thrilled to hear what I have to say, but guess what? That's on you. Imagine being such a shitty person that you're driven away from the police, of all jobs. That's like the mob telling you 'no thanks, you're too psychopathic for us.' Like, come on."

"You don't know a thing about what happened," Aksel growled.

"All right, then, why don't you share your side of the story with me, since you're making it so clear I don't know anything. Enlighten me."

"I can't tell you what you want to know."

"Oh, right, I'm just supposed to take your word for it."

Aksel's eyes bored into mine, and I looked bored right back, though I couldn't deny the crackling of electricity between us, the tension of two people who weren't going to back down.

"I'm telling you because you're innocent,

and you don't know what's going on. Stay away from this case."

"And I'm telling you because you don't seem to get it: you don't get to tell me what to do, and your opinion won't do shit to influence my actions. Now, get out of that chair before I pick up this scone and smear it all over your face. Which I don't want to do, because I'm really enjoying this breakfast, but that's how much you're annoying me."

"You wouldn't dare."

"You're not the first man who's said that to me," I said, curling my mouth into the most deranged smile I could and letting my eyes move out of focus. I really didn't want to waste half a scone. He wasn't worth it.

Aksel looked as if he was going to try and challenge me, but then he stood up. I smiled inwardly. In the battle of wills, I had won round one.

"All right, fine," he said. "I'll leave. But I'm warning you, be careful out there. The person who killed Greg is dangerous, as you've found out. I don't want you getting hurt."

"And I want to eat my scone in peace, without unsolicited opinions about my safety from someone I consider to be a suspect in this case," I replied.

Aksel shook his head. "I didn't try to kill you the other day. I told you I didn't."

"Ah, yes, famous people who always tell the truth, murderers. I thought you were leaving."

Aksel opened his mouth slightly, as if he was going to try and say something else, but he thought the better of it. He tapped his fingers against the back of the chair and walked off.

I flipped him the bird as he left but then realized this was the perfect opportunity to follow him. Where was Aksel going? What was he doing? This was my chance to find out more than the town's rumor mill had to offer.

As soon as the front door closed behind him, I jumped up.

"I'll be back," I called out to Sophie as I raced for the front door. But I stopped on a dime, raced back to the table, and grabbed the two halves of the scone that I hadn't eaten yet. Luckily, I'd put the jam and cream on before Aksel had come in. I caught Sophie's eye as she looked at me with a slight look of confusion. "For the road," I explained before racing off.

I could hear her giggling as I exited the coffee shop.

If Aksel had turned right when he exited, he would have walked past the window where I'd been eating, and I hadn't seen him as I'd grabbed my scones. So he had to have gone left. I raced down the street, taking a bite as I peered down every side street I passed. On the third, I spotted him. He was walking away from the sea, farther into town.

I followed him, keeping a safe distance behind. It was still early enough in the morning that there were no crowds on the street, no groups of people I could melt into and become just another anonymous face. I had to keep far enough away so that if Aksel turned, he wouldn't see me.

This cat-and-mouse game continued, with only one of us aware we were playing, for a couple of minutes. We were a few streets away from the coffee shop, into the deeper parts of town. There were stores at ground level here, with apartments above, but the narrower streets and dirtier sidewalks gave away that this wasn't the pristine, touristy part of town anymore.

Was this where Aksel lived? Was he going home?

A moment later, someone called out his name. "Evans!"

I paused where I was, around the previous corner, and pulled out my phone to see what was going on. I used it to look around the corner; I figured no one was going to spot just the three small cameras peeking around if they looked my way, whereas they would likely see my face.

The camera showed me what was happening straight away. It was Sergeant Peters and Inspector Hart. The two cops working this case.

I inhaled sharply at the sight of them all together. Aksel's shoulders tightened; he obviously hadn't planned on this meeting, either.

"What are you doing here?" Aksel asked. I could barely hear him; I was too far away.

Whatever the response was from Sergeant Peters, I couldn't make it out. I had to get closer. I needed to know what was being said.

Across the street, ten feet away, was a doorway set back a foot and a half or so into the wall. That would get me to within fifteen feet of the men so long as I could get there without being seen.

I shoved another piece of scone into my mouth, finishing off the first half of one, then gathered up my courage. I moved as stealthily as I could, being quick without being loud, shoving my body into the small recess in the wall. When I got there, I paused. Had I been spotted?

The sound of Inspector Hart's voice reaching my ears told me I hadn't. "You're not with the police anymore. You're not entitled to this kind of information."

I turned around carefully, still pressing myself against the wall, and listened in on the conversation, not daring to peek out and have a look.

"Don't play dumb with me, Jason. You know you need my help on this case. You're in over your head. I can help you."

So Aksel was trying to get the cops to share information with him. If he was the killer, that wasn't a bad strategy. Find out what they know so he could stay a step ahead.

"Bullshit. You always had such a superiority complex. We're doing fine on our own," Sergeant Peters replied. "I'm not going to break protocol by sharing information with a civilian."

The emphasis he placed on that last word, a slight sneer in the undertone, showed what he thought of Aksel no longer being on the force.

"Is that why you haven't made an arrest yet?" Aksel replied.

"You know damn well we can't just rock up to a suspect and throw them in prison. There are rules and regulations to follow, not that you care about that sort of thing," Sergeant Peters replied with a hefty dose of snark.

"Why are you interested in this case, anyway?" Sergeant Peters asked.

"I told you the last time, I've been hired to look into it."

"Hired by who?" Peters asked. "It doesn't make any sense. Gregory Hamlisch didn't have any family. No one who cared what he was up to."

"You're a detective. Figure it out."

Inspector Hart shook his head. "You're up to something, Aksel. I know you."

"Not as well as you thought you did."

"That's for sure. But I can tell when you've got something. What is it? Let us know. We can help."

Aksel barked out a humorless laugh. "Right.

Because I completely trust the Devon and Cornwall Police to do the right thing."

"You used to trust me to do the right thing," Hall snapped.

"'Used to' being a key phrase. You showed me exactly what kind of cop you were, and that's why you don't get the privilege of knowing what I know. Continue your own investigation if you think you're so good. You shouldn't need me."

"We don't," Sergeant Peters replied coldly.

"Hold on, who's that?" Hall asked suddenly, interrupting.

Uh oh. I was pretty sure I'd been spotted. My heart sank as the blood turned to ice in my veins.

"There's someone over there."

I heard footsteps coming my way, and I knew they'd spotted me. Damn it.

I still had half a scone in one hand and my phone in the other. So I turned on the video, put the phone in selfie mode, and plastered a huge smile on my face as I held the camera up high.

"And here I am now, walking through the streets of St. Albinus, enjoying a freshly baked scone. In case anyone asks, yes, I did put the jam on before the cream." I let out a fake laugh as I displayed my scone for the camera then panned around the street. "Now, the coolest thing about this place is the architecture. Look at these cute little buildings."

"Mackenzie," Sergeant Peters said, his tone

registering disapproval.

I spun around suddenly, looking at the three men in surprise. "Oh! Sergeant Peters. Inspector Hart. I didn't expect to see you here. I'm just making a quick TikTok video."

I tried not to focus on Aksel in the background but couldn't help glancing at him. What was that expression on his face. Amusement? He was enjoying this.

Asshole.

"Is that so? You just happened to be here?" Sergeant Peters asked.

"I did," I replied perkily, pretending not to hear the accusation lying beneath the surface of his voice. "It's such a gorgeous town. I was walking past with my scone, and I just couldn't let it pass by without taking a video. People are going to love it."

"Do you really expect us to believe that?" Sergeant Hall asked.

"Well, what else would I be doing here?" I asked innocently. I imagined Aksel was probably going to give me up, but given the tension between him and the cops, I figured I had a chance.

"For one thing, that's not the first building I'd choose as a backdrop when trying to record a TikTok video displaying the perks of the town," Sergeant Peters said.

I turned to take a closer look at the building I'd been hiding in the doorway of.

I'd been so caught up in spying on Aksel and the cops that I hadn't noticed what was sold in the store I was standing in front of. An old-style wooden sign hanging above the awning read, "St. AllPenis Adult Toys, Lingerie and More."

Around the words was a painted image of a man done in pre-Renaissance style, complete with a golden halo around his head, holding what was obviously a giant dildo in one hand. Great.

In the window of the store behind me was a poster for what I imagined must have been a recent release. A woman on the front, dressed in a sexy pirate's costume, looked surprised as a pirate ship rose in the background. The text on the poster read "The Pirates in Peg's Ass."

But hey, I was dedicated to this lie now. There was no way I was going to let the fact that I'd been pretending to take a TikTok video in front of an adult shop stop me from continuing with it.

"This was all part of the plan to go viral," I insisted, keeping my voice casual. "I'm taking my video here, and in the background, I intend for people to notice the poster. They'll point it out in the comments, it'll be seen as funny, and the next thing you know, I'm going to be TikTok famous with millions of views."

"That's crap and you know it," Sergeant Hall growled. "You were following us. Listening in on a *confidential* conversation."

"I had no idea you were there," I replied with a cheeky smile, knowing there was no way they could prove otherwise. "Why would I care what you do?"

"Because you killed Gregory Hamlisch, and you want to know how close we are to arresting you," Sergeant Peters replied.

I took a bite from my scone, taking the time to chew and swallow, which only seemed to make the cops madder. Hall balled his fists at his side, while Peters began tapping his foot impatiently. "I already told you I didn't kill Greg, and if you're still looking at me for it, that means you're that much further away from finding the real killer. Great police work."

I gave the men the fakest thumbs-up I could muster. In the background, Aksel smirked. Apparently, we had a common enemy. I was annoyed that my heart jumped a bit at the sight of his lips curling upward. There was a good chance he'd tried to kill me, so why was I still attracted to him? Talk about red flags.

"All right, we're obviously not getting anywhere here," Hall replied. "Get out of here, and stay away from our investigation."

"I guess I'll go record my TikTok videos somewhere else. I'll be sure to show you this recording when the real killer is caught," I said. Without another word, I turned and headed back the same way I had come, my heart racing in the aftermath of that whole experience.

Chapter 21

By the time I made my way back to the Ugly Mug Café, a few more people had wandered in, and Sophie was busy behind the counter, serving customers. But my table was still as I'd left it, and my coffee sat, mostly untouched, along with another half of a scone.

I sat back down and took a sip of the coffee, mulling over what I'd just heard while pulling out my phone and going through my messages.

I'd heard back from a few people about the tables and chairs and other random items I'd found that I thought would look good in the bookshop. I replied to the messages to organize pick-up times while I thought about what I'd seen.

Obviously, Aksel and Sergeant Peters had worked together. The way they interacted, I had no doubt that they knew each other, and I believed they knew each other well. They'd worked together and had a falling out, and it sounded like it had been over whatever had caused Aksel to leave the police force.

It was also interesting that they didn't know who had hired Aksel, either. There was no one obvious, and that added another point in favor of him being the killer. He could have made up having a client and have been using his job as an excuse to get close to the investigation.

"So," Sophie said, sliding into the seat across from me, interrupting my thoughts. She wiggled her eyebrows up and down. "Aksel, huh?"

I rolled my eyes. "It's not like that. Not like that at all. Besides, I think he might have tried to kill me, remember?"

"True. But that doesn't make him any less hot."

"You have a really messed-up sense of what dudes to be attracted to, you know that?"

Sophie shrugged. "You sound like my therapist. I know. Believe me. It's a problem. I'm actually an Aries, but I should have been born a Taurus given as I run straight toward every red flag I see."

I laughed. "I guess self-awareness is the first step toward fixing the problem."

"And it is a problem. Did you get anything good when you followed him?"

"Not as much as I was hoping for. Although I did see an interesting conversation. We'll see if it turns into anything."

"Did he see you? After all, if he shoved you off those rocks, he's dangerous."

"Not until there were more people around," I replied.

"Good. Shit, I don't like thinking about how close the killer is to getting to you."

I shrugged. "Me either, but there's no other choice, really. I have to, to get evidence."

"You're right. Okay, I have customers, but let me know if you need anything."

"Will do."

Sophie left, and I went back to organizing pickups. When I was done, I bussed my plate and cup then headed back out into the street.

I stopped by the hardware store and bought a few more supplies, which I left at the bookstore before going back home. I found Maggie sitting at the table, looking over the notebook I'd found in Greg's home once more.

"Anything interesting?" I asked, plonking myself down onto one of the chairs. Toast immediately tried to jump up, but the chair was a little bit too high for her small kitten body, and she hit the side of my leg before falling back down to the ground. I reached down, scooped her up, and placed her on my lap. She purred contentedly and began kneading biscuits on my thighs.

"Unfortunately, nothing new," Maggie said. "I thought perhaps giving the notebook another look after a few days might reveal something else, but no. I think the answer is in here, though."

"Maybe. I ran into Aksel Evans again this morning."

"Oh?"

"Even though he's not one of the gamblers on this list, I don't trust him. I still think it's all too convenient that I saw him just minutes after being pushed into the sea. And there's something that doesn't make sense. Who hired him? Why is he looking into this? He was speaking with Sergeant Peters and Inspector Hall earlier. They obviously know each other and don't like each other."

"That makes sense. They probably worked together before, when Aksel was one of them."

"My thoughts exactly. There's bad blood there. I don't trust him. There's something suspicious about him. He also came to see me at the coffee shop and tried to warn me away from this case. Under the guise of caring about my safety."

"And yet you think he could be the one who tried to kill you."

"I do. I don't have any proof, though. Also, I'm organizing with the sellers to pick up the items I wanted today."

"Good. I'll phone Dennis later and tell him we're looking to employ his services. In the meantime, why don't we pop by the butcher's and see if Kevin happens to be working?"

"Sounds like a plan. I'm meeting a new friend for lunch as well."

Toast had practically fallen asleep in my lap, and it pained me to move her, but we had a murder to solve. Toast mewled at us unhappily as we were leaving. It almost seemed as if she wanted to come with us. I was sure she'd love the butcher's, but unfortunately, a murder investigation was no place for a tiny kitten.

"So, who's the friend?" Maggie asked as we headed out.

"The woman who rescued me from the ocean."

"It's always a good idea to befriend the people who can save your life."

"My thoughts exactly. Plus she's interested in the case. She loves mysteries."

"Everyone interesting loves mysteries," Maggie said. "Our brains are designed to be curious."

"I agree. Although personally, I'd be very happy if I wasn't smack dab in the middle of one right now. There's more at stake when it's your own freedom on the line."

"But also more incentive to solve it," Maggie pointed out. "We're here."

The butcher shop was set back one street from the harbor. The street continued on, and through the gap, I could see the masts of boats, sticking up like white candles in the world's birthday cake.

Maggie and I entered the butcher's small shop. The ceilings were low, and everything was a little bit old-fashioned, but the display case was full of meats on offer. Behind the counter stood a guy who looked like he hadn't gotten any sleep in about four days. The dark bags beneath his eyes sagged heavily. His curly red hair sat like a mop on top of his head, and it had definitely been at least a week since he'd run a brush through it.

But the most surprising thing was that there was no way this kid was older than sixteen. I knew I was getting old, and it was getting harder and harder to tell how old kids were, but there was no way this was an adult. Absolutely no way.

"Can I help you?" he asked, his monotone voice indicating that there was nothing in the world he wanted to do less than help us out right now.

"I'll take two pounds of lean mince and a couple of pork chops," Maggie replied. "And I'd also like to know how much money you owed Gregory Hamlisch before he was murdered."

The guy was midway through opening a plastic bag when Maggie finished that sentence, and he paused to gape at her. "What?"

"You heard me. We know you're one of the people who was gambling with him. You owed him money. Eight grand, by our estimation, but we thought we'd rather hear it from you."

"It's because you're not eighteen yet, isn't it?" I chimed in, stepping forward.

The teenager's eyes darted between us. He obviously didn't know what to do.

I figured the more we pressured him right now, the more likely he was to tell us something that might help. "You weren't able to gamble through legal means, since you're not an adult, but Gregory didn't mind."

Maggie understood what I was doing and continued. "He told you that back in the day, everyone with the money could have a little punt, right? And he could front you the money. But it all went bad for you, and now you're stuck in a hole you can't get out of. So you went to see him a few nights ago, telling him you had the money. You decided to meet up in the bookshop, and when he got there, instead of paying him back, you plunged a knife into his chest."

The kid standing in front of us had gone so pale a part of me wondered if he was about to pass out from blood loss. "I... that's not what... no, I didn't kill him. I don't know him. Didn't know him. Gregory Hamlisch? Only heard the name for the first time the other day."

Kevin was a horrible liar.

"Wrong," I snapped. He was obviously off-kilter from our immediate accusations, and I figured pressing him further might get him to accidentally admit to what he'd done. "You did know Gregory. You were betting through him.

And guess what? We don't care about that. We only want to know: did you murder him?"

"No," Kevin cried, his eyes wide. "I didn't kill him. I swear."

"Where were you two nights ago?" Maggie asked immediately, not giving Kevin a chance to breathe.

"Sleeping. I was asleep. At home."

"Can anyone back that up?" I asked.

"My dad can. He was home. We stayed up together. Watched some footy. Then I went to bed. So did he."

"You could have easily snuck out in the middle of the night," I replied. "Yesterday morning, where were you?"

"School. School. I was at school. My teachers can confirm. I had maths first thing then science. But that's where I was."

"Okay, let's say we believe you," Maggie said. "You were betting with Gregory Hamlisch. Tell us about that."

Kevin looked behind us as if willing another customer to enter the store that he could serve instead.

Maggie placed her hands on her hips. "No one is coming to save you from our questions, Kevin. The best way to get out of this is to answer us honestly. We already know, you're just confirming information we already have. Gregory Hamlisch. You were betting with him."

"All right," Kevin admitted, running a hand through his hair. "All right, fine. Yes. I was."

"How did you get involved with him?" I asked.

"A friend of mine's dad was betting with him. That's how I found out about it. The friend said that Greg was willing to front money to people who needed it. People who couldn't place bets down at the shops for whatever reason."

"And your friend's dad, who is he?"

"Alfie."

Maggie nodded. "So you heard about this, and you thought to yourself, 'Maybe Greg would front some money to a kid who can't place bets himself because he's not eighteen yet.'"

Kevin took a deep breath. He was obviously starting to calm down. "Yeah. Yeah, that's right. I want to get out of here, you know? I graduate in a month. I want to go up to London, but with prices the way they are, there's no way I can afford it. I thought if I could make some money betting, I'd be okay. I'd have a bit of cash, and I wouldn't have to ask my mum for anything."

"But things didn't quite work out that way for you," I said quietly.

Kevin shook his head. "Look, no. They didn't, okay? You got me. It turns out it was a bit harder than I thought it was going to be to make money gambling. I'd put money on what I thought was a sure thing, and all of a sudden, in just one game, the team I was betting on would collapse. I started to feel like I was a bit cursed."

"And you got deeper and deeper into the hole," Maggie said.

"I'm not proud of it," Kevin admitted. "At first, I thought to myself I'd just make another play, and that would save me. I'd get there. I'd make the money back. But I just kept losing more and more. I'd make one good bet, and that would help, but then two bad ones would put me in a worse situation.

"Honestly, it's been bad. I was worried. I didn't know what to do. Greg was starting to come after me. Told me he was going to cut me off when I hit ten grand. That was fine, I was sure I wouldn't. My luck had to turn, and soon."

"You were convinced you'd actually climb out of the hole you made?" I asked, struggling to keep the incredulity out of my voice. Even after he'd lost eight thousand pounds of money he didn't have, Kevin still thought he was going to profit from this venture.

Kevin nodded. "Yes. I had a new strategy. I'd already made back one grand of the money I owed. I started doing the opposite of what I thought was right. If I thought a team was going to win, I'd bet against them. It actually started working. I'd figured it out. I'd solved the curse. I was going to work my way back. Then Greg was going to owe me money."

I blinked at Kevin a couple of times. Surely, I

hadn't been this stupid when I was a teenager. There was no way.

"So you see," Kevin continued, "I wouldn't have killed him. There's no way. Greg was going to be my way out. Not only was I going to make back the money, but he was going to owe me. My strategy was working. I just had to keep going."

"How long until you turn eighteen?" Maggie asked.

"Six months."

"Let me give you some advice, though I'm sure you won't listen. Never gamble again, you hear me? You got lucky this time around. Both men involved in this are dead. No one's going to come after you for the money they owed, but that's not going to happen once you grow up."

Kevin shook his head. "No way. My strategy worked. I know how to make money with this."

"You owed him eight grand, you dumbass," I said. "Sure, you made back a thousand bucks because you got lucky a couple times. But it's not going to happen forever. Gambling is designed to lose you money. Don't throw everything away."

"I don't have anything to throw," Kevin replied. "My parents aren't rich. They don't have the money to send me somewhere. When I graduate, either I'm making my own way in the world, or I have to stay in this dinky little tourist town, spending my days selling beef for barely enough money to pay for food."

"Gambling isn't going to get you out of this situation," I replied. "It's only going to make things worse for you."

"You don't know that."

"There's eight thousand pounds that say I do."

"She's right," Maggie chimed in. "We can't stop you, and I know you feel this is your way out. But I promise you, it's not. Stop gambling. You've got a problem, and you're not even legal yet."

Kevin scowled. "I didn't come here to be lectured by customers about how I live my life."

"You're only being lectured because you're making stupid life decisions. And this is coming from someone who's currently the prime suspect in a murder, so when even *I* know you're fucking it up, maybe it's time to listen," I snapped.

Kevin's eyes widened as he stared at me.

"We're only trying to help you," Maggie added.

"Look, thank you. But I've got it. Believe me."

"Yeah, I believe that as much as I think a unicorn shits across the sky to make rainbows," I replied.

"Do you know of anyone else who might have killed Greg?" Maggie asked. "When you spoke with him, did he tell you about anyone else who might have had problems with him? Threats? Anything like that?"

Kevin shook his head. "No. At least, not to him. He threatened me a few times. Said he was going to tell my parents if I didn't start paying my debts. I don't make a lot of money here, since I only work weekends."

"He didn't tell you he was going to break your kneecaps?" I replied.

Kevin shook his head. "I'd rather that than tell my parents, though. I'm not going to lie to you. Greg dying worked out really well for me. But I didn't do it. I'm telling you."

"Okay," Maggie said. "Now, how about you get that meat for us?"

"You're not going to tell my parents, are you?"

"Consider Greg's murder to be the luckiest thing that's ever happened to you," Maggie replied. "I'm not going to tell your parents. I'm just going to warn you. You made this mistake once. Don't do it again."

We left the butcher shop five minutes later, Maggie carrying the bag of meat.

"Do you think we need to confirm his alibi for my attempted murder with the school?" I asked.

Maggie shook her head. "There are toddlers with better bowel control than he had when we started asking him about Greg. There's no way that boy murdered him, or tried to kill you."

"I agree completely. Which means we've gone through the whole list of people in that

271

notebook, and we still don't know which one of them did it. Could we be on the wrong track? Was it someone who killed Greg for reasons that weren't related to gambling debt?"

Maggie frowned. "It's possible. I suppose it depends on whether or not Carl was involved in other aspects of Greg's businesses." She let out an almost inaudible sigh.

I tensed next to her. She was obviously struggling with coming to grips with this other side of her son's life. I imagined it would be difficult for any mother to learn about this sort of thing.

But knowing and not being able to do anything about it? Never being able to ask for an explanation? Never getting answers? That must have come with its own pain that she was trying hard to keep under wraps.

"Why don't I ask around?" I suggested. "I'll see what I can find out."

Maggie gave me a sharp look. "I know what you're doing. I don't need you to protect me from the facts."

"And here I thought I was being subtle."

"In case no one has ever told you, you're as subtle as a fart on a meditation retreat."

"Gee, thanks."

"I do think you're right, though. Either Greg was deeper into business with Dirk than we know, or someone is lying to us. There's also your attempted murder."

I shrugged. "Look, I realize I can rub people

the wrong way, but I don't think I managed to convince two different people to want me dead within seventy-two hours of landing in this country. Whoever shoved me into the water had to be the killer. Surely."

"Yes. I think that's a safe assumption to make. And it helps us to confirm alibis as well."

I sighed. "Which means we have the same problem as before. Okay, I'm going to go back to the bookstore and seal the floor. Feel free to go through all the papers I brought back yesterday if you think there could be something in there. I'll look too when I get back. I'll text you about pickup. I really hope it's obvious Dennis is our killer."

"Me too," Maggie said.

"Is there any way your network of locals can find out what the story behind Aksel is too?"

"If anyone knew anything, the whole town would be aware by now. I think that's a dead end."

"Too bad," I replied.

We split up then, with me going toward the bookstore and Maggie heading back home.

Chapter 22

I SPENT ABOUT AN HOUR SEALING THE FLOOR with a mixture I'd gotten from Wattle's, and when I was finished, it was time to meet with Ada. Then, afterward, I'd be using Dennis's services to pick up a few of the items I'd found online for the store.

When I entered the Ugly Mug Café, Ada was already seated and waiting for me. I ordered a sandwich and a cheesecake along with another iced caramel latte from Sophie at the front counter then went and sat down with her.

"You're looking better this morning," she said with a smile.

"Wait until you see me in my celebratory best once I actually find this killer," I replied. I caught Ada up on the whole case, and right as I was finished telling her the story, Sophie came by with all of our food and drinks.

"I swear, if I miss out on some key murder-solving here because we're busy, I'm going to be mad," she warned us jokingly.

"You're welcome to join," Ada invited her with a warm smile. "Whenever you get a chance."

"I will when things quieten down a bit."

When Sophie left, Ada turned back to me. "So, you're thinking Aksel is still a good suspect?"

"I do. I don't like not knowing what went on with the police."

"I can't even begin to help. I had no idea there was anything. I've only lived here a year."

"Yeah, so there's a university here? That's where you work?"

"It is. One of the oldest in England and one of the best for my particular line of work."

"Well, if you ever need any books, once I open my shop, hit me up. I'll give you any you need at cost."

"Thank you so much. That's a really kind offer."

"You save my life, and I'll take care of you however I can," I replied. "As long as the killer doesn't strike again. You might have to cash in those chips pretty soon."

Ada laughed. "I hope not. So you're thinking it's someone related to the gambling thing?"

I nodded. "It makes the most sense, apart from Aksel."

"I think it makes more sense," Ada said slowly.

"Why's that? What have I missed?"

"Well, the crime had to be premeditated."

I nodded. "Agreed. I doubt there was a set of knives just hanging around the bookstore, so the killer had to have brought it with them."

"My thoughts exactly. So that makes it more likely that the killer was the one who decided on the meeting place."

"Oh?"

"I think the killer was the one who set up the meeting. Think about it. If Greg had called someone and said, 'Let's meet here, at this place I use, and have a meeting,' they probably wouldn't have come with a knife. Especially if they didn't know what the meeting was about. Why would they? They wouldn't know that they had to kill Greg. But if *they* set up the meeting, knowing they wanted to kill him, well."

I nodded. "That changes things. Still, it's not a guarantee. Maybe the killer had a good idea about what Greg wanted. And they brought the knife just in case."

"It's possible," Ada admitted. "Still, I think it's more likely the killer set up the meeting. And who would do that? Someone with gambling debts who was used to going to the bookshop to pay them off. They would have suggested that place. Although maybe I'm wrong. After all,

Greg had a key. He might have thought it was a nice headquarters to use."

"There are just so many unanswered questions. But I'm going to meet Dennis this afternoon. Here's hoping he's wearing a T-shirt saying, 'I'm a murderer. Ask me where I hid the knife after I stabbed Greg.' I mean, okay, I know the knife was still in Greg's body. But still."

Ada snorted. "You can always hope, I suppose."

Sophie returned then and slipped into one of the chairs. "Hi, babes. I don't know how long I've got, but I want in on the murder chat. I'm Sophie."

"Ada," my friend replied.

"Ada saved my life yesterday. She pulled me out of the water after I was shoved in," I explained. "And she's spent her whole life reading mystery novels."

"Your favorites?" Sophie asked.

"Poirot," Ada replied with a grin. "I know he's a bit of a tosser, but I loved how he always let everyone think he was an idiot because he was a foreigner, and they'd always tell him things they wouldn't otherwise because of it."

Sophie grinned. "I approve. All right, what's the situation looking like?"

I shrugged. "Problem is, I don't have solid evidence pointing toward anyone. Maybe I'm just too nice, which is something that's never been said to me before. But I actually believe everyone we've spoken to when they say they're not the killer. So it could be Dennis, or it could be we're on the wrong track entirely by following the gambling. Or it's someone I've already spoken to, and like an idiot, I believed them when they told me lies to my face."

"And you're sure you've got the right list of people?" Ada asked.

"Yes. I found a whole notebook that was hidden in, uh, somewhere legal," I stammered. "The names were in code, but Maggie solved them."

"Great save on that lie," Sophie teased.

"Are you sure the code was solved right?"

I shrugged. "So far, it seems that way. He was using the last names of soccer players to refer to people's first names. So Norman was Hunter, because apparently there was a Hunter Norman who played soccer professionally here."

Sophie nodded. "He was one of my dad's favorites."

"That's how Maggie cracked the code. She knows all the players better than I do. And pretty much everyone has admitted that they were gambling with Greg when we confronted them. So she got it right. But we might be on the wrong track entirely."

"What about the murder weapon?" Sophie asked. "Any chance you can track it down? Find out where it came from?"

I shook my head. "The police have it, unfortunately. And when I had a chance to look at it on my own, that wasn't exactly my priority. You know, what with that being the first dead body I'd ever come across and all."

"I think that's fair enough," Ada agreed.

"So you can't do anything until you speak to Dennis," Sophie summarized.

"Pretty much."

A couple customers walked in then. "Okay, I'm going, but let me know what you find out from him. Ada, it's nice to meet you. We should make a group chat on WhatsApp."

"WhatsApp?" I asked.

"It's what everyone uses here for messages," Ada explained. "Download it onto your phone; you'll need it. Sophie, let me add you now, and then I can get Mack set up."

While Ada and Sophie swapped numbers, I opened my phone and downloaded the app. A minute later, Sophie was back behind the counter serving customers, and Ada was helping me get organized.

"You'll use this for basically everything," she explained. "It's the best way to set up group chat. Almost no one uses regular texts anymore in England."

"Good to know."

Ada grabbed my information and added me to their group chat. "There. Now you're all ready to go."

"Great, thanks."

"Of course. It's nice to have something to do. Life in Cornwall is great, but it can be a bit quiet sometimes."

"You said you went to Columbia, but you're new to Cornwall, so where did you grow up? London?" I asked.

"That's right," Ada replied. "Grew up in Peckham. My parents moved here from Nigeria before I was born. I love London, but I hate it, if you know what I mean."

I nodded. "That's how I felt about New York too. And Seattle, really."

"Some of my best memories are from London. The city will always hold a special place in my heart. But some of my worst memories are from there too. And with prices the way they were, it's become so difficult to live. You have to give up a lot to be able to stay there, and I don't think it's worth it if you don't absolutely love it."

"I completely agree. I always thought I would love New York. I'd hear all these stories about how crazy the city is. Full Thanksgiving dinner setups in the middle of the subway. Yelling at tourists walking three abreast on the sidewalk. Finding that tribe you really belong with. Making it in the big city, getting promotions, making a living, and eventually getting to the top of the corporate ladder. But reality was very different."

"What do you do for work?"

"I trained in marketing and went into advertising design," I explained. "I had a great job, and I was good at it. I worked in the internal marketing department for a large online retailer. Then, out of the blue, a month ago, I was fired so the company CFO's daughter could take my job."

"Oh, that's awful."

I took a deep breath as I tried to gather my emotions around the whole situation. "Yeah. I put everything I had into my job. I didn't have much of a social life, mostly by choice. I took pride in it, and then they just threw me onto the street, like it was nothing. I'm not going to lie: it hurt. A lot. And in a way, it felt like that was New York, you know? Where you can try as hard as you can to get ahead, and sometimes, it just dumps you on your ass anyway."

"It's tough out there. And with the economy the way it is too."

"That doesn't help. So when I got the letter telling me I had inherited a house and a store here in England, I was ready to jump all over that. I figured a change might do me some good. Moving somewhere I didn't know anyone. Living out the millennial dream of running my own small-town bookstore. But the millennial dream never mentioned the body."

"That would have put a bit of a damper on it."

"It has. But once the case is solved and I can

put it behind me, I'm going to open the cutest bookstore Cornwall has ever seen."

"I can't wait to visit."

"Thanks. How about you? You love it here?"

"I do," Ada said. "It's different, and there are things I miss about London, that's for sure. I have to make my own jollof rice, and there's nowhere in the world quite like Queen's Road on a Saturday, but I like being around nature. I love being able to step outside and know that I'm only a few minutes away from dozens of hiking trails. That I can get in my car and drive a few minutes, and if it's not summer, I can find myself completely alone, surrounded by nothing except the sound of nature.

"I do my research here, and it feels so much more organic when I can exist in the same world as my specimens. When I can just go out to the sea and find the right seaweed to do tests instead of having to order it in."

"I can see that being fulfilling."

"And the lifestyle here is a little bit more relaxed, you know? Everything moves slowly. New York City is the same as London. Everyone always feels as though they're racing toward the next goal. That if they stop moving for even a second, they're going to get held back."

"Yeah, I know exactly what you mean."

"That doesn't exist here. The people seem to understand that it's all right to take an extra couple of minutes to smell the flowers and enjoy the view. And I like that. Cornwall isn't perfect. Nowhere is. But as far as places I've been go, this is where I'm happiest."

"I'm hoping in a few weeks, I might be able to say the same thing."

"You will. You'll find the killer. I know it doesn't feel like you will at the moment, but every time you cross someone off the list, every time you follow another clue, you're getting closer. Eventually, it's going to click. You'll see what you've missed, you'll ask the right question, and it will all come together."

"If anything, I'm solving this out of spite," I said with a laugh. "No one gets to try and kill me and get away with it."

"That's the spirit," Ada said, grinning.

I meant it, too. It was one thing to kill Greg and try to ruin my life. It was entirely another to try and take *me* out. I was going to survive on spite alone.

Chapter 23

AFTER LUNCH WITH ADA, I SPENT THE afternoon organizing the items I had to collect with Maggie and Dennis. We decided not to confront him about the gambling until after he'd finished the work for me, and for a couple of hours, he used his truck to get around town, picking up a few tables and other items I'd found online.

He even helped to carry them from the road over to the bookstore, and by the time we were done, I was kind of exhausted.

"Thank you, Dennis," Maggie said, pulling out her purse after we'd dropped off the last items. "We really appreciate it."

"Happy to help a new local out," Dennis replied. He was in his forties and fit, dressed casually in jeans and a T-shirt. He had a couple days' worth of stubble, and his brown eyes were kind. He leaned against his truck—a newer black Toyota Hilux that looked like it would get stuck going down a few of the one-way streets in this part of the world. But Dennis had no problem driving it around.

Maggie handed him some bills, which he took. "Listen, while we have you, we also wanted to ask you about Greg."

"Oh?" Dennis asked as he counted the bills then shoved them into the back pocket of his jeans. "What did you want to know? If I killed him?"

"Yes," Maggie replied simply.

"If you're coming to me, you obviously know I owed him money, then. I didn't kill him, though his death was a nice bonus for me. Won't deny that. Didn't shove the knife in him, though."

"How much did you owe him?" I asked. We had the figures; I knew Dennis owed a shade over six thousand pounds. I just wanted to see if he would tell us the truth here.

"A bit over six grand. Not the smartest thing I've ever done, gambling through Greg, but live and learn. Well, not if you're Greg, I suppose."

"You're awfully open about your mistakes," I pointed out.

Dennis shrugged. "I don't think having a punt here or there is the sort of thing a man should be ashamed of. Nothing illegal about it."

"Apart from borrowing money to do it," Maggie said.

"True. But who's it hurt apart from me? I suppose Greg, depending on who killed him. But it wasn't me. I did bet with him. I openly admit that. I didn't kill him, though. I'd have paid him back eventually."

"You don't seem particularly upset that we just asked if you're a murderer," I said.

Dennis shrugged. "Someone killed him, didn't they? It makes sense you're looking into it, since from what I hear, the police think you two did it. Which is ridiculous, of course, but that's the police around here for you."

"Who do you think did it?" Maggie asked.

"A man like Greg? I imagine he has countless enemies. Could be someone else who owed him money. Someone who tired of him trying to scam them. Someone who simply needed him out of the way. You've lived here long enough to know what he was like, Maggie."

"He was found in the bookshop, though. Where you'd go to make the payments on your debts," Maggie said.

"That is true. And I'm sorry about Carl."

"Thank you."

Dennis continued, "I'd love to help you. Really, I would. As much as it helps me to have Greg dead, I'm not a big fan of killers walking the streets, free to murder whoever strikes their fancy. But I don't know who it was beyond telling you it wasn't me."

"Where were you the night he was killed? And yesterday morning?" I asked.

"Sleeping and at home. Alone. Why do you want to know about yesterday morning?"

"Something else we've come across. It doesn't matter," I replied.

"Well, I wish you luck in finding the killer. It wasn't me, though."

"All right, thanks," Maggie said. "We appreciate the help."

"Cheers."

Dennis climbed into his truck and drove off, and I let out a slightly dejected sigh.

"Oh, come on. It's not like he was going to admit to it straight up if we just asked him politely enough," Maggie said.

"I know. But still, a girl can dream. Do you like him for the murder?"

"No," Maggie admitted with a frown. "But it's possible he was so nonchalant about things on purpose."

"I just wish I knew more about Aksel. What was his link with Greg? Is he involved in this? I like him for this, especially if we've looked at all the people gambling and have ruled them out for one reason or another. Because otherwise, we're back to square one. I swear, I'm this close to going back out along the hiking paths to see if the killer tries to get me again, just to find out who they are."

"Personally, I'd rather you find another way

of solving this, all else being equal," Maggie said.

"Does that mean you're coming around to having a granddaughter?"

"As far as mysterious grandchildren go, you seem to be about the best a person could hope for. I'd have been quite disappointed if you turned out to be boring."

"I've never been accused of that," I replied with a grin. "Okay. We're officially looking into Aksel, then. Ask around and see what you can find out. I'm going to follow him. See what I can find out."

Maggie nodded. "Right. Are you staying here for now?"

"I am. I want to organize all this stuff I brought in. I'm thinking in a week or so, I might be able to reopen. Do you want to see it?"

"I'll wait until the grand reopening if you don't mind," Maggie said. I couldn't help but notice that this whole afternoon, she'd avoided going into the bookstore. It must have still been painful for her, seeing this place that had been her son's.

"Okay, no problem."

"Besides, I imagine Toast will be quite ready for a can of food back at home."

"True."

Maggie headed home, while I entered the bookstore and began setting things up.

I was interrupted after about an hour by a

phone call from the distributor Carl had used, which was a welcome distraction. I was able to keep the same account, and the woman on the phone set me up online so that I could place orders for any books I needed quickly and easily.

They delivered three times a week to Cornwall, which was great for me. I made a mental note to make a list of books I was going to need to order.

Heading to the back room, I began to set up all the books that Carl had ordered and kept in stock. The man obviously didn't know how to run a small bookstore. Instead of keeping one or two copies of a thousand different books in stock, he ordered like a Barnes and Noble. Why were there at least 50 copies of *Spare*, the memoir written by Prince Harry, on the shelves? He didn't need anywhere near that many copies. Not right off the bat.

I began organizing the books, sorting out what was going on display right away and keeping the extra copies at the back for now. I'd eventually run through them all, I was sure, but I wasn't going to put out thirty copies of a single book on the shelves. Especially since I now had way less shelf space than Carl had had when he ran this place.

Now, I only had the three bookshelves along the walls and three large tables that I'd bought from locals, one rectangular and two round. I set the rectangular table up below the window at the front of the store. The two round ones went in the middle of the space.

Between them, I placed a couple of upholstered chairs and a love seat that I'd also found being sold online. All in all, I'd spent less than two hundred pounds, and it made the store look cozy and inviting. I could have used another love seat for the other side of the store, so I made a note to keep an eye out for something suitable.

As I worked, putting books out on display, I ran through the facts of the case. Was Aksel the killer? If so, why? What was his motive? That was what I hadn't quite figured out. Could he have been involved in running drugs as well? Gotten on the wrong side of Greg?

I wasn't sure.

Eventually, I reached the whole collection of books Carl had collected about soccer. Of course, they were all by men. *My Life in Red and White. The Accidental Footballer. On Days Like These.* Almost all of the books sported large pictures of the men in question who either had written them or had written about them.

"This is bullshit," I muttered to myself as I opened up my phone. I'd been set up with an account to order books, so I typed "women's soccer" in the search bar.

Then I pressed the back button and replaced it with "women's football."

Sure enough, there were plenty of results. *Lioness: My Journey to Glory* by Beth Meade. *You*

Have the Power by Leah Williamson. *A Women's Game. The Pride of the Lionesses.* There was no shortage of books on women's soccer, and I was going to order a whole bunch to go with the testosterone-filled shelf Carl had set up.

Abruptly, I paused.

Something clicked. It was as if all of the puzzle pieces suddenly fell into place.

I knew what we had missed. I knew who had killed Greg.

Chapter 24

I RUSHED OUT OF THE BOOKSTORE AND ONTO THE street. I was right. I was sure of it. But how could I prove it?

I had to get evidence. It was one thing to know I was right, but I had to be able to prove it. But how? A confession would be the easiest way. Could I record one? Shit, I didn't know what the law was in England.

I pulled out my phone and mashed my question into Google. As it turned out, no. I could record someone without their knowledge but only for personal use. If I got a confession on tape, without them knowing about it, it wouldn't be admissible in court.

"Shit," I muttered to myself as I paced around the street. I must have looked like a crazy person, but whatever. Better crazy than killer. What was I going to do?

Then, it hit me. I was going to have to use

myself as bait. Exactly what Maggie had told me not to do. Well, I'd never been great at listening to instructions.

But I didn't have any other options. I had to do this. And I was going to come out on top. There was no doubt about it.

I paused, looking at my phone. I couldn't tell anyone else what I was going to do. They would just try and talk me out of it. I knew that. Besides, if there was one thing I'd learned in this world, it was that I couldn't trust other people. Not entirely.

I was doing this alone. I couldn't risk Maggie trying to convince me to get the answer some other way. This needed to end, and this was the best way to do it.

Taking a deep breath, I shoved my phone back into my pocket and set my plan into motion. The first thing to do was to hit up the Horny Goat.

Adrenaline had begun pumping through my veins the second I pieced everything together and realized I knew who the killer was. I had to force myself to calm down and try to walk normally down the street. I reached the pub and took a deep breath before stepping inside.

It was after six, which meant the pub was now bustling with energy, far busier than it had been the last time I'd come here, with Maggie.

Still, Dave noticed me from his spot behind

the counter and waved. I returned the gesture and walked toward him, looking around.

"All right, love?" he asked when I reached the bar.

I settled onto one of the seats in front of me. "Yeah, thanks," I replied. "I've had a long day of setting up the bookstore, and I figured that stew was so good I should come back for some more food. Can I get dinner up here at the bar, or do I have to wait for a table?"

"Ah, you'll have to get a seat. But go on, then. There's a few tables at the back still empty. Go ahead and take one. I'll let Chrissy know you're here, and she'll bring a menu right over to you. You'll order from her."

I thanked Dave and headed to one of the empty tables, with my back against the wall so I could check out the whole bar.

About a minute later, Christine arrived with a menu, which she handed me with a smile and a "Welcome back."

I perused the options, and when Christine returned a couple of minutes later, I ordered a diet Coke and the sirloin steak with onion rings. Because why would you ever have fries when onion rings are an option?

While I waited for my meal, I glanced at my phone. With the initial adrenaline rush of solving this case wearing off, I began to wonder if maybe I was going about this the wrong way.

What if things went wrong? Shouldn't I have some sort of backup, just in case?

No, not yet. I could do that later, but if I let anyone know my plan now, there was a chance it would be interrupted. I couldn't let that happen.

When Christine returned with my meal a few minutes later, I smiled at her. "Thanks."

"Of course. How's it going with the case?"

"Good," I told her. "I think I'm really close to finding the killer. I know why they killed Greg. The gambling thing that Norman was involved in? Yeah, I found a coded list of all the people who owed Greg money. They were all going to the bookstore to make the payments to Carl. That's probably why the killer met him there that night. To make a payment. It's just a matter of cracking that code and matching names. Then I'll have the killer dead to rights. I haven't shown Maggie the book I found yet. I was planning on doing that tonight. Hopefully, she'll be able to help."

"Good, I'm glad to hear you're getting close. It's scary, you know? Working here, my shift ends late at night. Eleven most days, midnight on Saturdays. Between closing up and getting ready for the next day, I'm not normally out of here until after eleven thirty, and sometimes it's closer to one o'clock. I've always walked home, and it's only ten minutes, but lately, I find myself looking over my shoulder constantly. I haven't been putting my headphones in and listening to music the way I normally do."

I shot her a sympathetic look. "I know exactly what you mean."

"Cornwall isn't supposed to be like the big city. You're supposed to feel safe here. Well, I'm glad to hear it. I hope you solve this case soon."

With that, Christine left me to eat my steak and think about what was going to happen next. I finished my meal, settled up the bill, then headed back out into the street. It was nearing nine o'clock now, and the sun had just dipped over the horizon. The sky was on fire, a pink glow coming from the horizon, which turned into a deeper blue with every passing minute.

It was going to be dark soon, the perfect weather to lure in a killer.

I hung around near the entrance to the Horny Goat for a couple of minutes after exiting. I was planning on being followed. I desperately wanted to look behind me, but I couldn't. I couldn't alert the killer to the fact that I knew they were going to be coming.

My heart pounded in my chest so loudly I was sure it could be heard from a mile away. I began to walk through the streets toward the park. It was getting dark; the tourists and locals who would have flocked to Politician's Point to enjoy the sunset would be making their way home. I expected it wouldn't take long before I was alone, and that was when the killer would strike.

I walked along the same path as the other day, and sure enough, I ran into quite a few people heading back toward town. By the time I got to Politician's Point, there were only a few people around, and they were obviously getting ready to leave.

I went to the lookout and gripped the railing. This morning, the sea had been a gorgeous blue. Now, as the night darkened, it had turned to an ominous black. The waves crashed against the rocks below, splashing up white foam as a warning.

Don't fuck with the ocean.

I had no intention of doing so at all.

After a couple of minutes, I stepped away from the security of the railing and walked closer to the edge of the cliffs. My stomach flip-flopped as I saw the water below. The memory of having been shoved in, of having nearly died, came flooding back to me. I swallowed hard, forcing it away.

I opened my phone and figured now was the time to send that text. There was nothing anyone else could do at this point anyway. I messaged Maggie.

I'm at Politician's Point. I think the killer is coming after me. If I die, you should know: it's Christine.

I set the phone to record and tried to open my ears to footsteps, to the signs of anyone coming after me, but it was no use. There was too much noise coming from the ocean. The waves crashing against the rocks. The wind roaring. The flapping of the flag on top of the lighthouse.

Instead, I steeled myself. I wasn't going to be caught unawares this time.

And about two minutes later, the attack came. Once again, I felt someone shove my shoulders. But this time, I was ready.

Instead of falling forward, I let the top half of my body crumple, bending over as if I was reaching down to touch my toes. I spun myself around and ran forward.

I tackled Christine like a linebacker, wrapping my arms around her knees. She let out a yelp as we both went crashing to the ground. I rolled off her and jumped to my feet, immediately ready to take her on.

"You knew," Christine snapped at me as she struggled to get back to her feet. In every movie I'd seen, ever, when someone was struggling to get up during a fight, the other person always let them do it. They gave them time to recover, time to get set for the next stage.

There wasn't a chance in hell I was going to do the same. "Damn right I did," I replied as I ran toward Christine and kicked her in the stomach.

She let out a groan, but she grabbed at my leg and wrapped her arm around it.

I let out a shout as I lost my balance and fell hard to the ground. Pain coursed up my left arm, and when I tried to move it, I let out a cry. Shit. This wasn't good.

Now I was the one who needed a second.

"You owed Greg money," I said. "Thousands of pounds. Twelve thousand."

"He threatened me," Christine said. "He told me if I didn't start paying him back, he was going to tell my parents. I couldn't have that. I couldn't let them know. They worked so hard, and they just retired. Dad was so happy. He was going to travel for the first time. They planned a trip to Santorini this summer. If Greg told them what I owed, they'd cancel it. They'd be so disappointed in me. I'd have ruined something else for them. I couldn't let that happen."

"So you killed him. You told him you were going to pay him back, and you asked him to meet you at the bookstore."

"He had no idea," Christine said, a deranged smile crossing her face. "I waited until I was close. Too close. But he was a man, so he took it as a compliment. And then I struck. You should have seen the expression on his face when he realized what had happened. He was shocked. Then he started bleeding, and it turned to horror. He was dead in seconds. Have you ever seen a man die?"

"No, because I'm not a fucking psycho who kills people."

Christine shook her head. "Neither am I. I had no choice. And then you started getting closer to the truth."

"So you tried to kill me. That's literally what psychos do."

"I didn't want to. I felt bad about it, really. They say drowning is one of the nicest deaths you can have."

"You know what's better than drowning? Not being dead," I snapped back. "Also, anyone who claims that it's a nice death has never been shoved into the ocean."

"Well, I tried. I wanted it to be as simple as possible for you. I thought it would get chalked up to the silly tourist, the new person in town who didn't heed the signs saying to stay away from the water. I didn't want you to die, but it had to happen. You were investigating, and I couldn't let you get to the truth."

"I wasn't just investigating. I figured it out. I broke the code. I knew it was you. That's why I went back to the Horny Goat for dinner. I wanted you to know I was on the right track. I wanted you to know I figured you out. I planned this."

Christine stared at me, surprise registering on her face. She hadn't realized I'd done this on purpose.

"Yeah, that's right. I figured you out, and I trapped you this time."

"How did you figure it out?"

"The names on the list. One was Sinclair. Maggie thought it was Jerome Sinclair, but I spoke to him. He told me he didn't gamble. I thought at the time he was lying, but in the bookstore I realized something. The natural assumption was that all of the soccer players he listed were men, but Christine Sinclair, from Canada, is one of the most famous women's soccer players."

"It doesn't matter," Christine spluttered. "You're still going to die. You have to die."

And with that, she rushed me again. My left arm was still killing me. I stepped out of the way at the last second and stuck out my foot. It connected with her ankle, and she fell to the ground, but before I had a chance to strike, she got up again and rushed at me.

This was it. Time for my Hail Mary.

I pulled the steak knife from the pocket of my jeans and stabbed.

I ordered the steak on purpose. I'd needed a weapon, and stealing the knife that came with my meal had felt like the best way to get one. I wasn't aiming for anywhere in particular; I just wanted to hurt her. The blade connected with something soft, and I grimaced as I felt it enter her body.

Christine pulled away, a horrified look on her face. I looked down as well. I'd stabbed her right in the stomach. I pulled the blade back out instinctively, and a patch of red bloomed in the center of her white shirt.

Christine clutched at the wound then looked at me with an expression of horror. Then, she launched herself at me.

Screaming, she ran toward me. I tried to stab her again, but she grabbed my hand and twisted my arm hard, making me drop the knife.

I tried to elbow her in the face, but I missed.

She took the knife and thrust it toward me.

The red patch on her shirt was growing, but not fast enough. I was back on the defensive.

Suddenly, Christine was illuminated by lights coming from behind me. An engine roared, and I instinctively turned to see what was going on.

A car was heading directly at us. The tires squealed over the ground, and it dipped and rose on the uneven terrain.

I gasped, gathering enough sense to dart out of the way, just as the car reached us.

Christine ran as well, heading in the opposite direction. She stumbled and fell. The last I saw of her was as she rolled over the nearby ledge and down toward the water.

The car screeched to a stop only inches from the cliff face. A second later, Maggie climbed out.

"The only person allowed to try and kill my granddaughter is me," she announced.

Chapter 25

MAGGIE AND I RUSHED TO THE LEDGE WHERE Christine had fallen. My stomach lurched as I looked down into the churning water below. This was different from where I had fallen. There was no nearby beach. The rocks here rose, black and ominous, jutting out of the water at least fifty feet high.

"She's not surviving that," Maggie remarked, voicing the thoughts I'd just had. "I suppose we'd better alert the authorities."

I pulled out my phone, which was still recording. "I have evidence of her admitting to the murder. It's not admissible in court, but it should get the police off our backs."

"Why didn't you tell me earlier you knew it was her?" Maggie asked.

"I didn't want you to try and stop me. I knew baiting her was going to be the only way to get her to admit to what she'd done."

"You could have told me. I would have helped."

"You did help. Massively. How did you drive the car here? There aren't any roads in this park, are there?"

"Roads are for rule followers. I go wherever this beauty will take me," Maggie said, patting the hood.

Right. I should have guessed. "You deserve to have your license taken away."

"My driving just saved your life," Maggie pointed out.

She wasn't wrong.

Maggie pulled out her phone and made a few phone calls. While she spoke with the authorities, I wrapped my arms around myself, wincing with pain slightly as I looked out at the water. Christine was in there somewhere. Probably dead. There was no way someone could survive that.

The sky had turned from navy blue to deep black before finally, the police arrived, flashlights in tow.

Sergeant Peters and Inspector Hart were first on the scene.

"What's going on here?" Peters asked, surveying the scene.

"It's as I reported on the phone. Christine attempted to murder Mackenzie. I arrived just in time to stop it, and Christine fell over the ledge and into the water."

"How did you get a car here?" Inspector Hart asked, looking almost impressed.

"Which one of you threw her into the water?" Peters interjected, looking between Maggie and me.

"Neither one of us," I replied. "She stumbled and fell. It was an accident."

"I don't believe you," Peters snapped. "You're both under arrest."

"I don't have the time or the crayons to explain this to you," I said. "But we didn't kill Christine. She's the murderer. Listen."

I pulled out my phone and began replaying the recording, fast-forwarding to the part where Christine admitted what she'd done, including admitting to trying to kill me.

Both men listened intently.

"There. So if you think you're going to get anywhere by arresting me, sure, go for it. But I have proof that Christine tried to murder me first. If you put either one of us in cuffs, I will not only put this recording on every single social media platform known to man, but I will personally make sure it's sent to reporters for every major newspaper in England *and* in America.

"And before you think to yourself that maybe you can get away with this by taking my phone, it's too late. I've already sent the recording up to the cloud. It's out there. So think long and hard about how this is going to come back down on you before you pull out those handcuffs," I snarled. I'd had enough of these dumb cops trying to pin Greg's murder on me.

Being a moron wasn't an excuse to try and ruin my life.

Maggie grinned. "Just in case you weren't sure she was one of mine, now you know."

"You've always been trouble," Peters growled at Maggie.

"And you've always been a man with a fork in a world of soup," Maggie shot back. "Now, you're going to let us go, and you're going to write your report that says Christine killed Gregory. Her body will probably wash up in the morning, or she'll be declared dead as well, and we'll all go about our lives as normal."

Inspector Hart nodded. "I think that's the most reasonable solution here."

"Good. I'm glad one of you seems to have a modicum of sense. Come on, Mack. Let's get out of here. This isn't our problem anymore."

Without looking back at the police, I stepped into the passenger seat of the car, knowing this trip back was going to be wild.

But nothing could compare to what I'd just gone through.

Maggie drove through the long grass, the car bouncing over the hills, the bottom scraping along the rocks that dotted the landscape. I clutched my left arm, holding it against me, wondering if every bobble was going to be the last for this car. There were ATVs that probably couldn't handle this terrain.

"Are you all right?" Maggie asked.

"Mostly. Something's wrong with my arm."

"There's no hospital in town, but there is a clinic."

"It can wait until tomorrow morning."

"If you're sure. Otherwise, I can drive you to Truro. It's about twenty minutes away."

I pulled out my phone and typed "Truro" into the directions. "That's funny, Google says it's thirty-five minutes away."

"That's because Google doesn't know how to drive."

"Yeah, Google's the problem," I mumbled under my breath.

Maggie turned and shot me a sharp look. "What did I say about complaining about my driving when it saved your life?"

"I know, I know. I'll be fine. I can survive until tomorrow."

A few minutes later, we were back at home. As soon as I walked in, Maggie had a look at my shoulder. "It's dislocated," she announced.

I winced. "That sounds bad."

"I need to put it back into place for you. This is going to hurt."

"Believe me, it hurts now."

"It's going to hurt more."

"I don't have a choice, do I?"

"Nope."

"Have at it."

I sat down at the small dining table and closed my eyes. Toast jumped up onto my lap straight away. I winced as Maggie took my arm in her hand. She pulled firmly, I felt a clunk, and immediately, the pain began to lessen.

"Oh, that's better," I whispered.

"Good. That means it worked. You'll need a sling. We can get you one from the chemist tomorrow."

Toast let out a meow as if telling me it was all going to be okay. And it would be. We'd solved the case. Christine was the killer. Maggie and I were no longer suspects. I could open the bookstore and live my life in peace, without this sword of Damocles hanging over me.

It was all going to be fine.

ONE WEEK LATER, I WAS INSIDE THE BOOKSTORE, anxiously shifting my weight between the balls of my feet, staring at the clock. It was two minutes to ten, which meant I had exactly one hundred and twenty seconds before I opened the bookstore once more.

Everything was perfect.

Toast was lying on her bed, which took pride of place on the rectangular table in front of the window. She could nap in the rays of sunshine that poured through or watch the comings and goings of the world. I'd been taking her in to work with me as I set up, and it was obviously her favorite spot.

The other tables and shelves were full of books. I'd placed a large order with my new distributor that had arrived a few days ago. Single copies of three hundred different books, which allowed me to fill the shelves with a wider variety of reading material.

Gone were the fifty copies of *Spare*. Instead, there were now copies of lesser-known books. Books I'd found by browsing Goodreads, watching TikTok videos, and looking at Instagram. These were books people read and loved, even if they weren't on the bestseller list, and I knew my customers would enjoy them too.

In front of the door were four dozen cupcakes, delivered by Sophie this morning, made by Ann. I'd ordered them a couple of days ago to celebrate the opening, and Ann had promptly refused to take any sort of payment for them.

Outside, the new sign Sophie had created stood out brilliantly. The Broken Spine. She'd done an incredible job with the sign, painting it a gold that contrasted just right with the dark-blue exterior.

One minute to go.

I looked around one last time to make sure everything looked perfect.

And it did. I'd found a couple of extra-cozy

chairs to place around the store. Ada had driven me to her favorite nursery, a small ways out of town, where I'd bought a handful of plants that added brightness and extra life to the space. My favorites were the asters, purple blooms with yellow centers that glowed brightly in the sun on the table near Toast, surrounded by books.

Ada had even found a flowering vine that I'd hung along the top of the bookshelf along the back wall of the shop.

The clock struck ten, and I walked to the front door, my fingers hovering over the latch for a second before I unlocked it and opened the door wide. The Broken Spine was open for business.

I turned and headed back inside, waiting for my first customer.

Two minutes later, a man walked in. Tall. Tousled hair. Carved cheekbones. Annoying, twinkling eyes. A frustratingly gorgeous smile.

My first customer had just walked through the door, and it was Aksel Evans.

BOOK 2 - AGAINST THE ODDS: MACK OWENS is happy to finally settle in and sell some books in peace by the Cornish seaside after solving the murder age was suspected of on her arrival. But you know what they say about the best laid plans...

When a friend of Maggie's dies, everyone believes it's by natural causes, including the local authorities. But Maggie knows better. Someone killed her friend, and she enlist's Mack's help to prove it. And just when Mack thinks a new murder to solve is enough for one week, she finds herself embroiled in the middle of a theft at a poker game involving many of the less savory characters in town.

And she's not talking about the Cornish pasties.

Unfortunately for Mack, Ansel and his twinkling eyes and annoyingly gorgeous smile seem to be her best bet when it comes to getting some of the answers she's after. But there's someone dangerous out there, too. And as Mack doubles down to prove Maggie's friend was killed, she realizes someone out there is intent on making sure she folds... permanently.

Against the Odds is available now. Find it at your favorite book retailer.

About the Author

Jasmine Webb is a thirty-something who lives in the mountains most of the year, dreaming of the beach. When she's not writing stories you can find her chasing her old dog around, hiking up moderately-sized hills, or playing Pokemon Go.

Sign up for Jasmine's newsletter to be the first to find out about new releases here: http://www.authorjasminewebb.com/newsletter
   You'll also receive the short story describing how Dot and Rosie from the Charlotte Gibson Mysteries met.s

You can also connect with her on other social media:

Also by Jasmine Webb

Mackenzie Owens Mysteries

Dead to Rights

Against the Odds

Blast from the Past (coming January 2024)

Charlotte Gibson Mysteries

Aloha Alibi

Maui Murder

Beachside Bullet

Pina Colada Poison

Hibiscus Homicide

Kalikimaka Killer

Surfboard Stabbing

Mai Tai Massacre

Turtle Terror (coming November 2023)

Poppy Perkins Mysteries

Booked for Murder

Read Between the Lies

On the Slayed Page

Put Pen to Perpetrator (coming August 2023)

Printed in Great Britain
by Amazon

41522741R00182